## "Something wrong?"

As Alex slowly turned to face Megan, his matted naked chest gleamed in the lamplight. Lazily he released the catch of his belt buckle.

"What are you doing?" she asked, sternly ordering herself to breathe at a normal rate, keep her voice on an even keel and hold his gaze.

"Getting undressed. We spies don't like to sleep with our clothes on."

Megan heard the snap give way on his jeans, then the raspy sound of the zipper being lowered, and she felt a shiver of both anticipation and apprehension. "Uh, is that standard operating procedure?"

"Give me a break, sweetheart. It's not like you've never seen a naked man before."

His thumbs hooked in the sides of his open fly, Alex peeled the jeans down his hips and, despite Megan's attempts to keep her gaze in the relatively safe territory above his waist, her eyes drifted downward. Though she felt her face heat, she couldn't look away before making two very telling observations.

This particular spy wore nothing under his jeans but bare skin.

And he wasn't exactly as immune to her as he might pretend to be....

**Sheryl Danson** grew up watching "I Spy," "The Man From U.N.C.L.E." and *every* James Bond movie ever made. So it's no surprise she made the hero of her second Temptation novel a spy! Add lots of sizzle, humor, a gutsy nineties heroine, and you have another winner from this Pennsylvania native. Sheryl also works part-time at her local Waldenbooks store. "All those wonderful published books serve as inspiration to write more!" she quips.

**Books by Sheryl Danson**

HARLEQUIN TEMPTATION
434—ALWAYS A FIANCÉE

# THE SPY WHO LOVED HER
## SHERYL DANSON

**Harlequin Books**

TORONTO • NEW YORK • LONDON
AMSTERDAM • PARIS • SYDNEY • HAMBURG
STOCKHOLM • ATHENS • TOKYO • MILAN
MADRID • WARSAW • BUDAPEST • AUCKLAND

ISBN 0-373-25579-9

THE SPY WHO LOVED HER

Copyright © 1994 by Sheryl McDanel Munson.

# 1

"YOU HAVE GOT TO BE kidding," Alex Sullivan growled. His caustic tone clearly indicated that he was considerably more exasperated by what he'd just been told than he was skeptical about the truth of it. "How *does* that woman manage to find her way to every hot spot in the world just as all hell breaks loose?"

"I don't think she does it deliberately," Frank Baker, Alex's immediate supervisor, answered reasonably, despite his perception that trying to reason with Alex on that particular subject was pretty much a wasted effort. "Or, for that matter, just to aggravate you. She's an archaeologist, for God's sake. It's inevitable that her work takes her to Third World countries, many of which are unstable enough to erupt at anytime."

"In the last ten years, the Agency has had to get that woman out of Nicaragua, Iraq, Ethiopia, Cambodia, mainland China . . ." Alex's irritated tally of the countries, all of which had been subject to periodic bouts of unrest during recent years, was marked by a series of brief pauses as he ticked each one off on a rigid finger. "And wasn't she in Armenia for the earthquake?"

"You're blaming her for natural disasters, now?"

"I never said she was *responsible* for any of them," Alex forced out through gritted teeth, his green eyes blazing angrily. "I'm just pointing out that that damn woman has a truly remarkable talent for ending up in the wrong place at the wrong time. And every time she does, we're the ones who have to go in and get her out of there in one piece. Can't we revoke her passport?"

Frank chuckled, thoroughly amused by Alex's uncharacteristic agitation. He'd noted, years before, that "that damn woman" also had a truly remarkable talent for punching all of Alex's buttons, and she didn't even have to be in the same hemisphere to do it. Frank didn't understand the phenomenon, but found it fascinating nonetheless. It was an impressive achievement, casting more than a few doubts on the long-held Agency-wide contention that Alex Sullivan had ice water in his veins instead of blood. The same had been said of Alex's father, an Agency man before his retirement to his Texas ranch. While Frank had never been able to figure out whether that characteristic was genetic or had been instilled in Alex since birth—or both—he was positive the old man must be proud of his progeny. Most of the time.

"Restrict her visa? Put her on a leash?" Alex continued, apparently on a roll. "Can't we at least send her a bill?"

Frank was unable to contain his amusement any longer and his chuckle erupted into a hearty roar of laughter. "I'd like to see you try."

The comment elicited a reluctant snort as Alex tacitly admitted the absurdity of the suggestion. They could both imagine what she'd say to anyone presumptuous enough to try and restrain her, even if it was for her own good. She could curse fluently in no fewer than ten languages, any one of which she'd be more than glad to demonstrate. Alex shifted in his chair, got up and began prowling the well-worn path in front of

Frank's desk. "But why do I have to be the one to go and get her this time?" he demanded.

"Because you know the region," Frank replied with a casual shrug. "Because you're good at jobs like this. Because you're available. And most importantly..." His pause was calculated to ensure he gained Alex's undivided attention. Settling his lanky height against the edge of his desk, he delivered the point that would conclusively bring the debate to an end. "Because I say so."

Alex scowled at the older man, who was even taller than he was, bristling at the less-than-subtle reminder that he wasn't nearly as independent as he liked to think he was.

"C'mon, Alex," Frank cajoled, enjoying the conversation more with each passing moment. He got so few opportunities to be entertained at Alex's expense, he intended to take advantage of this one while it lasted. "Lighten up. It's a piece of cake. All you have to do is fly over to Zoman, take the back way up to the ruins of Umal, grab her, and then scoot out again."

"Avoiding not one, but two, hostile armies on the way," Alex muttered under his breath.

"You could do it with your eyes shut."

It sounded so simple when Frank put it that way. Hell, it *was* simple, or at least it would be if that damn woman, Megan Davies, weren't involved. Alex sighed wearily, knowing none of his objections, no matter how vociferous or how valid, was going to be enough to alter his boss's decision to send him to Umal. Nothing less than the absolute, unvarnished truth could possibly change Frank's mind, and nothing less than torture would induce Alex to divulge *that*. "What the hell is she doing there, anyway? She was in the Peloponnesos, last I heard."

"The Aegean," Frank corrected patiently, resisting the urge to ask why Alex kept track of her whereabouts, since he was dead certain that the younger man would refuse to tell him. And he'd be damned if he'd give Alex the chance to defy his authority yet again over something so relatively trivial. "Himeros, to be exact," he continued. "Her team said they found some sort of ruins there that reminded her of something she'd seen at the Umal site—"

"And the next thing anyone knew, she went haring off alone to take another look at it," Alex completed for him. "Never considering for a single instant that she was heading smack into the middle of the latest escalation in the Zomani civil war."

"Basically." The scenario was familiar enough to both of them, because it had happened at least a couple of times a year for the past ten years.

Damn woman. *Damn plumbing*. He'd bet his pension it was plumbing. It always was. Alex sighed heavily. "All right. I'll go." As if he really had a choice. "When do I leave?"

TWO HOURS LATER, Alex was in the air aboard an Agency jet that was, by all appearances and according to every scrap of its official paperwork, the property of Crater Petroleum Products of Oklahoma. In reality, the ostensibly legitimate company was the product of the Agency's fertile imagination and limitless resources. Although he'd had no choice in the matter and was already on his way, Alex was still grumbling—to himself and the pilot and anyone else who would listen—about how much he didn't want to go.

His continued grousing notwithstanding, it hadn't occurred to him earlier to suggest to Frank that they leave Megan there to fend for herself. It would have been insubordination of the most flagrant kind, to say nothing of the fact that he wouldn't want to have to straighten out the godawful mess that was bound to result if either Zomani army ever got its hands on her. And, he admitted to himself, he couldn't bear the thought of Megan meeting with such a grisly fate.

It didn't make a bit of sense, but he couldn't help feeling some twisted sense of responsibility for her, even after all these years. It would just make his life one whole hell of a lot less complicated if one of the other men went and got her this time, next time, and every time after that, because he didn't want to see her, ever again, as long as he lived.

# 2

As HER RELUCTANT rescuer deplaned in Tel Mapur, the capital of Zoman, drove for two bumpy hours in an ancient Land Rover, and then set out on the four-hours-by-foot trek through the mountains to Umal, the intended rescuee was happily oblivious to any danger. What was important to Megan Davies was the evidence she'd found confirming that the Romans *had* occupied Umal at about the same time as they had colonized the Island of Himeros in the Aegean. It was a thrilling—and possibly significant—discovery.

All right, Megan admitted to herself, so it wasn't the Ark of the Covenant or Akhenaton's tomb or the Holy Grail, but, contrary to the image nurtured by Hollywood, archaeology was seldom glamorous. Instead, it was mostly a lot of grubbing around in the dirt, hoping to find something—anything—even if it was only the charred remains of an ancient fire ring. In comparison with a clump of long-dead embers, finding an entire sewage system was something big, something to get excited about, as was being in Umal for the first time in several years.

When the Romans had founded Umal as a colonial outpost of the Empire, they had utilized the natural caves that riddled the mountains, living and working in them as if they had been constructed for just that purpose. Additionally, they had hewn beautifully lav-

ish architectural facades out of the rocky mountain itself.

*More practically, they'd constructed a sophisticated
system of municipal plumbing,* Megan thought as she
clambered over a loose pile of rocks and crouched to
inspect the rubble. While to a layman, it would have
appeared to be worthless detritus, the way it crumbled
in her hand assured her it was some variety of concrete, the ancient Romans' favorite building material.
After placing a few samples in a plastic bag, she paused
to listen to the menacing rumble of far-off thunder she'd
heard intermittently yesterday and again today.

Neither the relentless heat nor the continual blue of
the sky eased her worries about stormy weather ahead.
She'd spent too many years working in just such vast,
remote sites to forget how deceptive distances could be.
The sound of thunder could echo across the open ex-
panses, giving little indication of how far away its
source might be, and the accompanying storms were
capable of moving with astonishing swiftness. Allowing herself to be lulled into complacency by apparent
good weather was not merely foolish, it could be dangerous, as well.

Like most other places that didn't get rain on any
regular basis and then got it by the buckets when it did
come, Umal had rocky soil that was more apt to chan-
nel water than absorb it—and if the furrows she'd seen
were any indication, the water would be channeled
right into the mouth of the pass through the mountains. In its simplest terms, Umal was a flash flood
waiting to happen, and Megan didn't want to be there
when it did. Things being what they were in Zoman
these days, who knew how long it might be before any-

one even remembered she was there, let alone got around to rescuing her?

AS HE FINALLY MADE his way up into the mountains, Alex found the thundering disturbing; he had no illusions about its cause or likely consequences. To him, the sound of gunfire was both unmistakable and ominous.

Picking his way from rock to rock and shrub to shrub, Alex kept up a steady litany of silent-but-imaginative curses, all of them leveled at the "damn woman" responsible for getting him into this fix. While it did absolutely nothing to rectify the situation, venting his spleen had a morale-boosting effect that did a great deal to dispel his sense of foreboding.

The reassuring effect lasted only until Alex passed through the last gateway into Umal, when his discomfiture resurfaced with a vengeance. Neither the magazine articles he'd read nor the ground plans he'd committed to memory during his flight had prepared him for the experience of *being* in Umal. It was, as the articles maintained, incredibly awesome, but it was also incredibly ominous, making his skin crawl in a fashion that had nothing to do with either the proximity of two hostile armies or the all-too-imminent encounter with Megan.

Alex assured himself he'd appreciate the magnificence more if he weren't alone. Umal was so big, its facades loomed over him, making shadows as deep as those of skyscrapers. And so old, it appeared to have stood there unchanged since the beginning of time. And so silent, it seemed as if even the most insignificant forms of life had been spirited away from the city along with its former inhabitants. He combed his memory for the location of the plumbing system's major components, knowing that that was where he'd find Megan. Even more than he wanted not to see her again, he wanted to locate her so they could get the hell out of here as soon as possible. Immediately would suit him just fine.

While he didn't find her immediately, it didn't take him very long to do so. That it required none of his highly-refined intelligence skills both distressed and infuriated him. It was appallingly obvious that either the Zomani government regulars or the freedom fighters or, for that matter, any other interested party could have located her just as quickly and effortlessly. All they would have had to do was follow the sound of vintage rock-and-roll to its source.

As he stood at the top of the hill on the outskirts of the ruins, Alex scowled down at Megan and wondered, for at least the thousandth time in the past fifteen years, how she had managed to survive for so long. Not only did she constantly blunder into places and situations anyone in his or her right mind would avoid like a nest full of angry rattlesnakes, she didn't even have the good judgment to be cautious about it. The music from her tape player—Bachman-Turner Overdrive's "Takin' Care of Business," of all things—was so loud, she might as well have posted big signs with arrows, like the ones his mother and her neighbors put out when they were having yard sales. In Megan's case, however, the signs would have to bear the legend: This Way To The Stupid American Woman. Any Day, Any Time.

He shuddered, imagining what fate might have be-
fallen her if someone other than himself had found her.
She was a blue-eyed blonde, all alone in a country
where blue-eyed blond women were merely a prized
commodity on the black market. Though he'd never
done any scientific research on the subject, he didn't
doubt that nearly-six-foot-tall blue-eyed blondes were
such a rare piece of merchandise; they were damn near
priceless.

Indeed, those legs would be enough to make her
damn near priceless almost anywhere. They were so
amazingly long, they seemed to go on forever—a qual-
ity that wasn't at all diminished by the rumpled shirt,
loose olive shorts, and scruffy work boots she was
wearing. Although presumably her clothing was cho-
sen for its serviceability rather than its alluring quali-
ties, it also, he was sure, would give any man with
active hormones an almost-irresistible craving to slide
his hand inside the wide leg of her shorts and up as far
as his arm could reach. That errant thought made Alex's palms itch, and he wiped them against the thighs
of his jeans in a futile effort to relieve the sensation.

He remained where he was for several minutes, during which his exasperation with Megan escalated at
nearly the same rate as did his desire to touch her. In a
valiant bid to rein in those unruly emotions before he
did something stupid—shaking some sense into her silly
head and ripping off her clothes were both high on the
list of possibilities—he cleared his throat with a low
cough not meant to reach Megan's ears.

In the two days that had passed since she'd entered
the uninhabited mountains surrounding Umal, Megan
had gotten so used to the absence of live human sounds

that not even the exuberant interference of BTO, the undisputed kings of party music, was enough to prevent her from hearing the distinctly live, decidedly human announcement that she was no longer alone. With a startled gasp, she tilted her head up to look toward the crest of the hill. At first, all she could see was a dark male shape against the bright backdrop of the setting sun, and a pang of terror shot through her as she recalled, in entirely too much detail, every bit of blood and gore and depravity from every horror movie she'd ever seen.

That emotion lasted no more than a split second before she was seized with the determination not to behave like one of the idiotically submissive victims in those films. Tamping down her fear, she rocked back onto her heels to confront her prospective assailant and discovered, too late, that her feet were both asleep. Caught off guard by the tingling sensation, she lost her balance, tumbled back, and landed solidly on her bottom, sprawled out with her hands behind her in a spiderlike posture that was both vulnerable and undignified. Coincidentally, the new perspective enabled her to identify the man at the top of the hill.

*Alex.*

While it had been almost five years—four years, ten months, and fourteen days, to be exact; dear Lord, why had she come up with that number so fast?—since she'd last seen Alex Sullivan, Megan would have recognized him anywhere, even with his face concealed by shadows as it was. The very silhouette of his body was imprinted on her memory as intimately and immutably as her own name. For a moment, her mind contended that the sight was some sort of hallucinatory apparition brought on by incessant heat and days without human contact, but then she acknowledged that it was real. *He* was real.

Given her druthers, she'd much rather have kept on believing he was only an extremely vivid figment of her imagination. Forget the old saying about "the devil one knows"; as far as *she* was concerned, no mere sociopath, either real or imagined, could possibly pose as great a threat to her as the one man who didn't just know the deepest, darkest, dirtiest secret from her past; he also embodied it.

That thought sent a wave of panic coursing through her, the likes of which she'd felt only twice before in her life. On both occasions, the sensation had been generated by her keen awareness that, if he got it in his head to be vindictive about it, Alex was more than capable of making her sorry she'd ever laid eyes on him in the first place.

In all truth, it was far too late for that. She'd already been sorry for the biggest part of the past fifteen years.

Though every instinct Megan possessed urged her to run for cover before she could find out if it was, in fact, possible for her to become even sorrier, instinct couldn't surmount the paralysis that gripped her as Alex stepped down from the embankment and came toward her with a long, predatory stride.

As she gaped up at the advancing figure, a single shaft of light edged under the brim of his hat, washing over his face. Sphinxlike and impenetrable, his facial expression—or, more precisely, the lack of it—gave her so little indication of what he was thinking, she might as well have been trying to read Linear A, the alphabet used by the ancient Minoan inhabitants of Crete. Lord knew they were equally lost causes, with no one as yet claiming to have found the key to deciphering either one.

She couldn't stop herself from making the attempt, however, any more than she could control the surge of emotions that swept over her an instant later. They ran the spectrum from desperation to defensiveness to desire and were, by now, as predictable as the panic; somehow, though, their intensity still managed to surprise her. She'd always thought she might have enjoyed them, too—if only she had ever detected any sign that Alex was similarly affected by her own presence.

She didn't now. And she never had.

A lot sooner than she would have liked, he was looming over her, taking off his sunglasses to reveal eyes as opaque as the dark lenses. Crossing his arms over his chest, he shook his head and heaved a deep sigh before he finally observed, "Some things never change."

They certainly didn't, Megan had to agree, though to be accurate, Alex didn't look precisely the same as he had five years earlier; he looked better. Despite all the hazards associated with his occupation, time had been kind to him. His hair—a sun-washed shade somewhere between blond and brown—didn't show a trace of gray, and the faint lines radiating from his brilliant green eyes were sun squints rather than markers of the aging process. Though his body had filled out a bit, it had retained its lean hardness, with muscles that were purely functional rather than just for display. He didn't look as if he *worked out;* he looked as if he *worked*.

The cumulative effect of the package remained the same. He still made every nerve in her body vibrate, and it took all her willpower not to reach up and touch him...or worse yet, drag him down onto the rocky soil beneath her. She hated herself for that weakness, as well as for her inability to keep the notion from being reflected in her eyes, thus telling Alex a great deal more than she wanted him to know. His soft chuckle of masculine amusement left her with no doubt that he could read her thoughts, and she scowled at his effortless ability to accomplish something he knew she couldn't emulate. No one, except maybe God, could read Alex's inscrutable mind.

Because staying where she was made her feel entirely too vulnerable, Megan scrambled to her feet, pulled herself up to her full height, and still had to look up at him. His stony countenance never wavered, even when she demanded, in the haughtiest "Queen of the World" voice she could manage, "What the hell are you doing here?"

The imperious tone had always been effective enough in dealing with the most insubordinate subordinates, auditors who understood a lot less about archaeology than they did about the bottom line, and maître d's at some of the snootiest restaurants on earth. With Alex, it failed miserably.

"I happened to be in the neighborhood . . ." he began, sounding so unrattled, she could have cheerfully murdered him and left his body for the vultures.

"And just thought you'd drop in and say hi," she snapped.

"More or less." He shrugged indolently. "Any objections?"

*Hundreds. Thousands.* "Not a one, as long as you aren't thinking of staying."

"I needed a vacation and the hotels in Cannes were all full. And Beirut just isn't the same anymore—"

"Alex . . ." she growled.

He ignored the warning. "—since they turned waterskiing into a duck shoot. So I asked myself, 'Where do I know somebody I haven't seen in a while?' And I thought, 'Megan's in Zoman. I guess I'll—'"

"Cut the crap, Alex, and get to the point."

"Cut the crap?" he repeated levelly, his eyebrows arching lazily to his hairline. The hummphing noise he made next might have been annoyance or amusement . . . or something else altogether. With Alex, they were all so similar, it was difficult to tell. "Me? Who the hell do you think you are, telling me to cut the crap when you're the one who's so full of it, you ought to come equipped with hip boots and a shovel?"

For the briefest instant, Megan impishly considered, and soundly rejected, suggesting that Alex might not be the innocent victim he considered himself. She fervently wanted to bait him until she hit a raw nerve and proved he had one, but she wasn't quite sure she was prepared for what might happen when if she succeeded. Given Alex's attitude on the subject of emotional expression, making him lose his temper would surely be an offense that would outweigh all her earlier sins put together, even if she thought it really would be good for him to find out he was only human.

Besides, Alex's question was all too close to the one she didn't want to face. She'd had reasons for what she'd done. Valid ones. She just wasn't sure she wanted to have to explain them to Alex.

"But then, they say if you stand in it long enough, you don't smell it anymore, don't they?"

She ground her teeth together, endangering thousands of dollars' worth of orthodontia.

"And trust me, Megan, there's one very pungent aroma of the barn around here."

"Dammit, Alex . . ." she muttered, glaring at him as if looks could kill.

"Dammit, Megan . . ." Alex echoed in a voice much calmer and more controlled than hers, meeting her eyes with a enigmatic gaze that would have done Clint Eastwood proud. He knew very well what she was doing.

*Attempting to do,* he corrected mentally. Now that she'd regained her equilibrium, she was every bit as prickly and guarded and determinedly cool as he'd ever seen her. The effort she put into the performance was admirable; it might even have been believable—if he hadn't seen her initial reaction first. The expression on her face hadn't been merely unguarded; it had been altogether transparent, revealing every thought and feeling that had passed through her mind since the moment she'd become aware of his presence. By the time the unruly tangle of her emotions had run its course, he'd come to the conclusion that things might have been a lot different if she'd been that honest with him years before.

She hadn't, though. She never had been.

All right, so she wasn't thrilled to see him again, exactly. The Lord and Megan alone knew why. There was definitely *something* still there. That certainty made Alex want to crow with laughter, throw his arms around her, and kiss her until they were both dizzy, and only a very small part of that ambition could be attributed to the satisfaction he always felt when one of his theories was proved correct.

For the time being, he checked the impulse to find out if Megan would still kiss him back the way she had when they'd spent spring break together in Florida. The aftermath of that youthful vacation and their two other encounters in the fifteen years since then provided him with plenty of memories for incentive to repress his reaction.

There had been Nicaragua, five years after Florida, in what would turn out to be only the first in a continuing series of Agency rescue missions. From the moment he'd found her until he'd left her at the base camp with the rest of her team, she'd been so full of meaningless hostility, she could have taught both sides of the conflict down there a thing or two about their specialty.

Five years after that, there had been Paris, at an embassy party where he'd been doing security duty. Actually, he'd been doing penance for ignoring orders in Rhodesia—the fact that later developments had proved him right notwithstanding—and Megan had been a guest. When he'd run into her at the hors d'oeuvres table, she'd acted as if he were no more than someone she'd met just in passing so long ago that she barely remembered him. He'd seen right through the sham and would have called her on it, but she'd run for the hills before the entrée had been served.

And now, she was back to meaningless hostility again. If that was the way she wanted to play it, he guessed he'd just have to accommodate her.

They stood toe-to-toe, challenging blue eyes glaring up into complacent green ones. Electricity arced between them, and neither noticed the last chords of Kansas's "Point of Know Return" fading away or the tape player clicking off automatically. For several very long moments a strained silence hung between them, until it was broken by a distant rumble that reminded them both that they had problems far more immediate and portentous than thrashing about in the last lingering debris of their first encounter.

They turned, peering off in the direction of the resonant sound, trying to determine how far away it was.

Finally, Megan frowned and muttered, "Damn. I don't see any clouds yet, so I still can't tell where it is. Can you, Alex?"

He pivoted toward her and stared at her profile incredulously. "Clouds?"

"Rain clouds," Megan clarified, though it seemed clear enough to her. Still staring off into the distance, intent on discerning the present location of the incoming storm, she hadn't seen the stunned expression on Alex's face, nor had she registered the corresponding intonation in his voice, both of which would have shocked her to her toes. "I've been hearing thunder on and off since yesterday, but there hasn't been a drop of rain yet." She sighed wearily, lifted one hand and raked it through her short cap of sweat-dampened hair. "Not that I want a monsoon or anything like that. God knows, this place couldn't handle it, but we could really use a break in the heat. Lord, it's been like an oven up here."

"Rain?" Alex parroted again, forcibly checking the tempting selection of curses that came to mind and resolving not to let her drive him over the edge, despite her apparent efforts to do precisely that. He closed his eyes, counted to ten, and then swallowed before answering in a carefully neutral voice, "Thunder? Is that what you *really* think that is?"

Alex's question brought her up short and she hesitated before squeaking, in a voice a full octave higher than her usual range, "Guns?"

"Very good. You had another guess coming, too."

"But they were all the way over on the other side of Tel Mapur when I came up here!" she protested, as if the assertion itself could make it a reality.

"Well, they aren't anymore," Alex sarcastically pointed out. A moment later, the full implications of her claim hit him with the force of a pipe bomb being detonated beneath a compact car. "You *knew* they were there?"

"I *knew* they were a hundred miles away," she snapped. "I figured they'd stay there a few days, at least, until I could get up here and back out again. Got any idea who's retreating?"

"Does it really matter?" In spite of his earlier resolution not to let it happen, Alex was so unnerved by her disregard of the danger that he was on the verge of losing control.

Megan pondered the question for a moment, which was entirely too long to suit Alex, before answering, "Not to me, since I have a hard time making up my mind about whether totalitarians or fascists are worse.... You, of course, don't have to deal with that sort of confusing dilemma, because you're behind the Agency line, whatever it is at the moment. By the way, which side are our tax dollars backing this week?"

His only visible response was a fierce clenching of his jaw. Megan allowed herself a small smile of feminine triumph. "And, anyway, it doesn't really matter, because I have letters of safe transit from both sides."

"Both?"

"Though there isn't much they agree on, both the government and the rebels—"

"Freedom fighters," he corrected automatically.

"Oh? So we're supporting them this week, are we?" she asked in a voice that implied she knew a great deal more about the American covert aid than was public knowledge. "At any rate, both of them are pretty gung ho about preserving their national heritage, which I study. And since I don't work for a museum or collector or anyone else who'd want to take valuable treasures out of the country, neither side feels threatened by me."

The convoluted yet inarguable logic of her explanation, as well as her apparent access to information usually available only on a need-to-know basis, left Alex speechless, because it refuted everything he'd ever believed or said about Megan. All along, he'd maintained it was her naïveté about other people and the world in general that got her into these messes time after time. As assumptions went, it had always seemed to be a valid enough one, convincingly explaining the way she ended up smack in the middle of one political and civil disruption after another, with any number of natural disasters thrown in just to keep things from getting predictable. Coincidentally, it had also provided a reasonable explanation for the ease with which he'd seduced her.

The evidence that she wasn't nearly as naive as he'd always imagined brought all those accepted principles into question. He didn't know why this evidence of her astuteness surprised him, because he'd always *known* she wasn't stupid, no matter what claims he'd made to the contrary. Somehow it surprised him to learn that she didn't meander blindly into one perilous situation after another without giving a thought to the risk; instead, she apparently walked into them with her eyes wide open, well aware of the potential dangers and at least marginally prepared to deal with them.

And that revelation gave him yet another reason to wonder exactly *who* had seduced *whom*.

# 3

BEFORE ALEX HAD TIME to consider that confounding question, another barrage of gunfire reminded him that they were standing on an open hillside without so much as a miserable blade of grass for cover. That kind of exposure went against everything he was *supposed* to have learned during years of Agency training. How could he have overlooked such a potentially lethal situation?

Megan, of course. Every time he saw that damn woman—hell, every time he heard her *name*,—his brain went AWOL, as if it didn't want to be held accountable for anything the rest of him did. Silently chastising himself for letting it happen yet again at a point in his life when he should have been old enough and smart enough to know better, Alex caught Megan's wrist, and began towing her toward the crest of the embankment. As they went, he briskly snapped back at her, "Got a camp? Where is it?"

Given the choice between following Alex or saying goodbye to her lower arm, Megan snatched up her camera and tape player and scrambled after him. It wasn't easy; for a man who didn't know where he was going, he was moving awfully fast.

"You picked someplace secure, I hope? With good cover?"

The questions were coming fast, too. He wasn't giving her a chance to answer a single one. And it didn't look as if Alex really expected answers—at least, not from her. Instead, she got the distinct impression he was consulting some higher authority—one a lot higher than her.

Now, *that* wouldn't surprise her in the least. As far as she could tell, *everyone* who worked for the Agency was convinced he had a personal understanding with the Almighty.

Minutes later, after her third attempt to pass Alex had led nowhere except to failure, Megan dropped back behind him again. Though admitting defeat, she was thoroughly annoyed by his refusal to recognize that sense occasionally outranked even divine sanction.

"Please, God, just tell me she didn't bring one of those fluorescent-orange tents with her," Alex muttered.

While her derisive snort would have quelled that concern, she knew he couldn't hear it, caught up as he was in his consultation with whatever powers might be listening. If any were, they weren't answering.

"Well?" he prompted sharply, coming to a halt so suddenly she stopped just short of running into his back.

*Finally,* she thought with some relief as she juggled the camera and tape player, struggled not to fall on her face, and admired the solidity of the back that was inches from her nose, all at the same time. *And before we get to the Persian Gulf, too. There may be hope for him yet.*

Once she'd recovered her hold on her valuables and her equilibrium, Megan confronted Alex with a level stare, and waited for him to figure it out.

"Well?" he repeated impatiently. "You gonna answer me or are we gonna stand out here until somebody shoots us?"

As if in response to his demand, a shell exploded in the distance; caught up in their own clash of wills, neither so much as glanced in the direction of the sound.

"Kinda hard to lead when you don't know where you're going, isn't it?" she observed.

"Dammit, Megan . . ."

Her gaze slid down to her wrist in a silent but unmistakable request to be released. A moment later, as his fingers relinquished their grasp, both Megan and Alex took note of the oval smudges left behind on her fair skin.

Remorseful at his unintentional heavy-handedness, Alex cradled her wrist in his hand and lifted it to inspect the damage he'd done. With his thumb, he gently chafed at the shallow indentations, as if trying to erase them. He only wished he could. Megan wasn't, by anyone's standards, a petite woman, but she was slender . . . so delicately slender, his fingers had overlapped as they'd encircled her wrist. When he considered how little additional pressure it would have taken to break the fragile bones, the thought made him queasy.

"Lord, Megan, I'm sorry," he breathed. "I didn't me—"

Checking his apology midword, she quickly shook her head and retrieved her arm. "No real damage." Not unless she counted the aftereffects of the soothing way he'd caressed her wrist once he'd realized what he'd done. Every nerve in her arm tingled from his touch, a sensation that seemed unlikely to abate anytime soon. Unconsciously, she rubbed her wrist in a fruitless attempt to make it stop.

Alex noted the gesture and frowned, wondering if he'd hurt Megan more than she was willing to admit. It wouldn't surprise him; past history had shown that the straight truth wasn't her strong suit. Opting to let the subject of her wrist—and a few other things she'd been less than honest about over the years—ride until later, when pursuing them wouldn't mean taking the chance of getting more directly involved in the Zomani civil war than either one of them or the Agency or the State Department would appreciate, he gruffly asked, "You said you had a camp?"

Megan gestured with a lift of her chin. "Back in the city."

He raised both hands, transferring leadership rights to her. "Lead on, then. After all, you're the one who knows where we're going."

Deciding it would serve no earthly purpose to point out that she'd tried to tell him that only moments before, Megan silently set off down the slope and into the city of Umal. Once she'd passed the fallen columns and chunks of stone that were all that remained of the forum—a combination marketplace and town square—she turned toward the group of caves that had served as homes for the Romans.

The cave she was heading for, the one in which she'd spent the previous night, had become her favorite the last time she'd been in Umal, mostly because she'd been captivated and amused by the paintings on its walls.

She couldn't call them unique, exactly. Prosperous homes throughout the Roman Empire had often boasted murals, with subject matter as diverse as still lifes with fruit and lewd Bacchanalia. What they had in common was the function of adorning an otherwise-plain surface ... and a graphic—or pornographic—dedication to illusionistic detail.

While Umal's wall paintings were as painstakingly accurate as the others, interior decoration didn't appear to be the Roman's sole objective. Instead of oranges or orgies, they depicted windows overlooking lifelike Italianate gardens; even the tabby skulking in the ferns around the birdbath was so realistic, it made her want to shoo away the sparrows before they became lunch. For years, she'd contended their purpose had been to alleviate the claustrophobia the caves must have induced in at least some of the residents. She herself had no problem with either enclosed spaces or the dark. She had enough other weaknesses, however—chief among which was right behind her, close and quiet as a shadow but a great deal more difficult to ignore—to feel compassion for those who did.

As a general rule, Alex had never been much of a follower, but he thought he could get used to it if a view of Megan's backside was always part of the deal. Like most tall women, she didn't wiggle a lot, but the sway of her long, leggy stride was incredibly provocative ... as was his sudden recognition that the smooth curve of female behind wasn't marred by any sign of a panty line. It was a riveting discovery, one he'd be glad to spend some time investigating, and there was no point in pretending his interest had a blessed thing to do with national security.

Megan's hips shifted again as she took another step, which pulled the fabric tauter across her bottom. His body responded to the sight, effectively demonstrating that his interest didn't have a thing to do with duty, either. His mind went AWOL again, leaving his body at the mercy of his hormones, and he couldn't, for the life of him, recall why he'd expended so much energy trying to talk Frank into sending someone else to get Megan out of Zoman.

With all his attention fixed on that question—and Megan's missing panty line—Alex was transformed into a paragon among followers: content, compliant, and completely oblivious to where they were going...right up until they actually got there. When Megan finally stopped, however, it was in front of something that looked like a porch, except porches didn't come attached to mountains, and they didn't have open doorways chiseled into solid rock. They weren't supposed to, anyway. As he looked up at the colossal facade, Alex assured himself it couldn't be true. Megan couldn't have been intrepid enough, or crazy enough, to make camp in the abandoned caves of Umal.

Just then, his mind became functional enough for him to recognize the obvious. She not only *could* spend the night in the cave, she *had*.

As Megan reached inside the mouth of the cave, retrieved a battery-powered lantern, and turned it on, Alex focused on the good news, such as it was: There was no longer any reason to worry about how to camouflage a fluorescent-orange tent. Hot on its heels, however, came the corresponding bad news: There was a bigger reason to worry, and that was that Megan fully expected him to go into the cave with her.

In order to keep Megan in sight once she stepped inside, he craned his neck around the edge of the doorway and peered into its dark depths. As she went farther into the mountain, her light grew dimmer and smaller, until all he could see were reflections on the ceiling and walls and the shadowy contour of her body against them. Even as he admired her lack of anxiety, a pridefully masculine part of him recoiled at the fact that it was very shortly going to become evident to Megan that he had some…qualms…about going into the cave himself.

It wasn't a phobia, Alex silently and firmly maintained, ignoring all prevailing evidence to the contrary. Phobias were nothing more than illogical, unreasonable fears weak men used to squirm their way out of unpleasant things they ought to do, when the shrinks weren't milking them for every BMW and vacation home in Aspen and Aruba they were worth. His…"misgivings" about caves didn't meet any of those criteria.

He'd never let that difficulty stop him from doing what he'd had to do, either; on the mercifully few missions involving caves, he'd suppressed his reaction through self-discipline and sense of duty—and done it well enough that no one in the Agency had ever gotten a hint of it, he might add. He'd done it before, and he could do it again…just as soon as he had a few minutes to pull himself together and talk himself into it.

Before he'd done either of those things, however, Megan was back. "Aren't you coming in?"

Alex shook his head, a bit too quickly for the movement to qualify as perfunctory. He assured himself that his ..."aversion" to caves was neither illogical nor unreasonable. He had reasons. Valid ones. He just wasn't sure he wanted to have to explain them to Megan. "I thought I'd stay out here for a while."

"But you're the one who said we had to get out of the open," she argued, clearly mystified by his sudden change of mind.

"I'll be along soon. You go on in."

"But ..."

"Dammit, Megan," he snapped. He'd forgotten how persistent she could be.

Megan frowned, obviously considering his uncharacteristic agitation. "You're claustrophobic?" she guessed, with a pleased surprise that made Alex think about handing her over to either the Zomani army or the freedom fighters—in this case, it really didn't matter which—for target practice.

"I am not claustrophobic," he denied. "And you know it. Remember that VW Bug? Cars don't come any smaller than that tin can on wheels. Remember that elevator in the hotel—"

"So it's just caves, then," Megan interrupted, before he could continue. He was probably going to remind her about the shower stall that must have been designed for use by gnomes. Gnomes who only took their showers one at a time.

"Caves can be *very* dangerous places."

Alex sounded so earnest, Megan was torn between hysterical laughter and just plain hysteria. The discovery that there was something in this world actually capable of scaring big, bad Alex Sullivan couldn't have come at a more inconvenient time. After leaning her back against one of the pilasters that flanked the cave's entrance and curbing the impulse to point out that he spent most of his time in places that were far more dangerous than any cave ever could be, she ventured, "Dangerous?"

"Do you know how often caves collapse?"

*Is he serious?* These caves had been standing, intact and without disturbance, for at least two thousand years. But Megan tactfully decided to keep that observation to herself.

"Mmm-hmm."

"And do you know how many people get lost in caves every year?"

*Is he serious?* Though it was undoubtedly possible to get lost in the caves, she only intended to go as far as the rooms that had once been houses for the Romans, not into uncharted territory.

"Mmm-hmm."

"And do you know how many kinds of venomous cave-dwellers there are in this world?"

*Is he serious?* The spiders and bugs, small rodents—some with wings—and lizards that lived in the cave were all things a man the size of Alex ought to be able to handle . . . especially a man with the extensive defense training his job required.

"Mmm-hmm, Alex . . ."

"And . . ."

*To hell with diplomacy.* At the rate this was going, they could both be blown to bits long before Alex ran out of rationalizations. While Megan couldn't help but enjoy the unprecedented evidence of Alex's discomfort, death and dismemberment were too high a price to pay for that privilege.

Telling herself that *he* had said they had to get out of the open—and hoping he'd remember that later, after he realized what she'd done—she assumed a smile that was much too ingenuous to be sincere and asked, "Are you going in there under your own steam, or do I have to knock you out and drag you inside?"

For a second, his eyes widened with something that might have been panic, but he tamped the emotion down with a stoic determination that she was forced to admire even as it irked her. He showed no sign of moving, and she told herself she should have known better than to expect success on the first try.

"The ground's awfully rocky," Megan tried again. "You might hit your head on something if I do."

He stiffened perceptibly and paled visibly beneath his tan.

"And you're heavy. I might drop you. Who knows what might break if I did?"

"Megan . . ."

While his knees were still locked, his color came back and the apprehensive look in his eyes was gone, replaced by a dazzling emerald gleam. She was sensible enough to recognize the warning in his gaze, but also sensual enough to appreciate its intensity, its fire, its—

*Don't be ridiculous,* she told herself. *It's nothing but cold, hard stone, and you know it. Anything else you think you see is just a figment of your imagination.*

"Damn." Levering herself away from the wall, she picked up the lantern again. "I'm not staying out here all night. If you are . . . well, that's up to you. See you in the morning." Turning back into the entrance, she added, "I hope you brought your own food and a way to cook it. There isn't a real tree—at least not one big enough to use for firewood—between here and the Lebanese border."

For the second time in ten minutes, Alex watched Megan enter the cave. When the light from her lantern was reduced to a speck in the distance, she finally spoke again. Just one word, in a voice scarcely louder than a whisper.

"Chicken."

The word reverberated inside the long black confines of the tunnel and then echoed several more times inside his head. Even more than he hated the way it sounded, he hated the way it felt. Acting on that thought so quickly he didn't have time to rethink it, Alex stepped into the passageway.

When he caught up with her, Megan automatically reached for his hand. His skin was cold and clammy, his pulse hammering as if he'd just run a marathon. Quite unexpectedly, she felt a pang of remorse at being the one to prove that Alex Sullivan wasn't as tough as legend—either the Agency's *or* the one in his own mind— would have it. She repressed the thought, assuring herself that in this instance, the end had justified the means . . . no matter how mean it had been.

And it had been. Mean, that is. After all, Alex had been born and bred in Texas, the state that invented machismo. He worked for the Agency, the organization that had perfected the concept and elevated it to a science. A good hard shot to his masculine ego was hitting him right where he lived, getting results neither logic nor sympathy could ever obtain. In a last, well-aimed blow at that fragile element—though she'd al-

ready attained her intended goal and knew perfectly
well it wasn't fair to kick a man when he was down—
she just couldn't resist asking, "You do like chicken,
don't you?"

The answering silence was so taut, it actually reso-
nated, and Alex's hand clenched over hers. While Megan was positive she was missing her once-in-a-lifetime
opportunity to see Alex show genuine emotion, she
thought she'd pushed her luck enough already and
didn't dare look at him.

When the light from the lantern fanned out in the
relatively wider spaces of the chamber a few minutes
later, Alex began to breathe easier; noticing the change,
so did Megan. She'd started to worry that he wouldn't
get better once they were in the living area, which
would have forced her to knock him out anyway...but only as a last resort, in case of imminent
heart failure. That resolution didn't mean she was entirely convinced that Alex *had* a heart to fail; her belief
in its existence was substantiated only by the presence
of his pulse.

As Megan tucked the lantern into a niche high in the
wall and Alex situated himself on one of the stone
"couches" that lined the periphery of the room, the silence of the cave loomed tensely between them. Intending to fill the vacuum before one of them did or said
something reckless, Megan popped a tape into the
player and turned it on.

*Big mistake*, she groaned inwardly a moment later.

She would have been better off with silence than with
a chance selection as chancy as Leo Sayer's "When I
Need You." Alex and old love songs were the last combination she needed, especially now. Against all logic

and the strident warnings of her better judgment, Megan was quickly coming to realize that she *liked* his unforeseen vulnerability almost as much as she enjoyed it. It made Alex more sympathetic, more human... and, worst of all, more devastatingly attractive than ever.

*Maybe he's mellowed with age.*

Even before the suggestion was fully formed in her mind, Megan told herself not to believe it. Hadn't she already seen, before they'd gotten to the cave, that Alex hadn't changed a bit? This was simply a temporary aberration, one that would end just as soon as they got out of here and he could go back to being his same old infuriating self.

Still, as she went digging in her backpack for dinner supplies, Megan couldn't help imagining what it might be like if she could hold Alex prisoner in here for the rest of his life.

From his seat on the bench, Alex watched Megan prepare the meal with a brisk competency he was forced to respect, even as he resented it. This...problem with caves was merely the kicker in what had already been the most galling twenty-four hours of his entire life. He was used to being in charge of a situation, and he hadn't been in charge of this one since the moment Frank had told him he was going to Zoman.

When he hadn't been bitching and moaning about how much he didn't want this assignment, he'd been fantasizing about what might happen once he got there. He'd envisioned himself charging in to save Megan, like every hero ever immortalized in history or legend. Sir Galahad and the Lone Ranger, because the symbolic imagery of white horses appealed to him. Robin Hood and Zorro, champions of the weak and downtrodden. Superman, defender of truth, justice, and the American way. While the details within the scenarios had varied, the endings had all been the same: Megan, grateful for his heroic rescue, had thrown her arms around him and rewarded him in the most elemental feminine way.

*Talk about leading a wild fantasy life.*

In addition to the fact that Alex hadn't counted on caves being involved, he'd overlooked the point that there had never been a woman less suited to play the role of damsel in distress than Megan Davies. She was neither helpless nor grateful; and the way things looked now, she was undoubtedly going to save *his* ass from the Zomanis before it was all over.

God, he hoped it didn't come to that.

"Dinner's ready."

Megan's announcement interrupted his thoughts, but the meal itself gave Alex new reason to resent her. Not only could she do everything else, she could cook, too, overcoming the handicap of prepackaged camping foods and a little solid-fuel burner with a handful of herbs from a plastic bag. It would have made him much happier if the meal had turned out to be absolutely inedible, but it was good. Good enough to annoy him immensely.

"So how do you like the paintings?" Megan asked as they ate, with Linda Ronstadt's "That'll Be the Day" playing in the background.

"Paintings?"

"On the walls." She gestured around them with the hand that wasn't holding her fork. "They're a little faded, but that's to be expected, considering how old they are. Earth colors, the reds, browns, and greens, particularly, get that way after a certain amount of time. Yellow practically disappears."

Really looking around for the first time since entering the chamber, Alex couldn't help smiling, in spite of himself. The paintings depicted windows. With gardens. Outside. If he'd noticed them earlier, they might have helped him get a handle on his untimely complication. At the very least, their existence would have assured him he wasn't the only person in history with an...aversion to caves. "One of these wouldn't be a way out of here that doesn't involve that tunnel, would it?"

She shook her head and laughed. "'Fraid not."

"Damn. I should have known it was too much to hope for." He looked around again and then broached a subject he'd wondered about before, one that was rapidly becoming an immediate concern. "Um...what about the, uh, facilities in here?"

Megan laughed again, and the seductive sound of it almost made him forgive her. That beneficence only lasted until she pointed toward the back of the room, to a shadowy place the light from the lantern couldn't touch, let alone penetrate.

"There's a real, honest-to-God bathroom back there. Wait'll you see the tub. It's big enough for a party of twelve."

"Gives a whole new dimension to all the stories about Roman orgies," Alex commented drolly, stalling for time until he made up his mind whether or not he actually wanted to seek out the bathroom alone. He considered the alternatives, none of which seemed practical or dignified.

"There's no water in the tub, and the toilets don't flush anymore, but . . ."

"Maybe I could just wait until morning." He paused a beat, as what she'd said sank in, and then stared at her. "Flush?"

She nodded. "The Romans invented flush toilets and municipal plumbing, you know."

He'd been right on the mark about the plumbing connection, but the realization gave him no satisfaction at the moment.

"You could leave a trail of bread crumbs to mark your way back," she suggested helpfully. *Too* helpfully, he thought, giving her a withering look that made it clear he didn't consider it a viable option.

Later, Alex couldn't have said what anything looked like between the main living room and the bathroom. Neither detours nor sight-seeing had been on his itinerary, which consisted of getting there, taking care of business, and retracing his way without getting lost en route. In spite of that no-frills approach, he had managed to note that the tub was even bigger than Megan had claimed, bordering on classification as a swimming pool. He'd rated its maximum capacity at somewhere between sixteen and twenty adults, depending on exactly how friendly they all were.

Though that observation suggested a range of possibilities almost beyond reckoning, he hadn't had a chance to cultivate more than one or two of them before getting back to the main chamber. At that point, any vicarious pleasure he might have derived from them was eclipsed by the expression on Megan's face. Her earlier amusement at his expense had been rankling enough, but she was now verging on full-blown hilarity at his nervous haste, and it didn't look as if she was trying very hard to restrain herself.

As Megan headed breezily off on her own foray into the back of the cave, Alex glared after her, his resentment rising to new heights. He might be a little slow on the uptake where Megan Davies was concerned, but he wasn't completely uneducable. Not even legs that were capable of launching a thousand male fantasies could negate the fact that that damn woman could also be more abrasive, devious, and evasive than any other woman he'd ever known.

And, this time, he wasn't letting her get away with it.

# 4

IF THERE WAS ONE MORE thing that could go wrong before she got back to Himeros, Megan didn't want to know what it could be. What had started out as a simple little excursion to collect a few samples of concrete had grown more and more complicated since the moment Alex Sullivan had arrived on the scene.

Not that she blamed him for the Zomanis' sudden notion to move the action up into the mountains, the Agency's decision to send him, or even the fact that his one and only weakness had put in its appearance now. She just would have been grateful if he'd managed to get there early enough in the day for them to head out of Umal before dark. While she didn't doubt his contention that making the trek at night would be risky, the prospect of dealing with Alex's unforeseen—and decidedly un-Alexlike—phobia in direct conjunction with bedtime didn't sound any safer to her.

In an effort to give him enough time to get himself tucked into his sleeping bag and fall fast asleep before she returned from her own trip to the back of the cavern, Megan dawdled considerably longer than necessary. When she finally returned to the main room, however, she thought she should have stayed away even longer. Though she'd meant it when she'd assured herself she was *not* about to repeat the same mistakes she'd made years earlier, it would have been much easier for her to maintain that resolve if Alex had fallen asleep while she was gone. In a tight voice, she asked, "You want to leave the lantern on all night?"

Alex smiled. While Megan genuinely wanted to be encouraged by this sign that his self-control was winning its battle over his dread of the cave, it reminded her, somehow, of crocodiles. "You can turn it down, if you want."

But did she? The lantern's lowest setting was an awful lot like candlelight, which was far too cozy to suit her, especially with Boston crooning "Long Time" in the background. With a quick mental note that she *had* to start checking the lists on her tapes *before* putting them into the player, Megan shut it off and turned to adjust the lantern.

As the light dimmed, a soft rustling noise behind her broke the silence, but, to Megan, it seemed louder, more recognizable, and infinitely more alarming than the sound of gunfire. Whirling around to face it, she silently reiterated her resolution, along with all the reasons she ought to keep it.

That concern hadn't just been unwarranted, she realized at once; it had been ridiculous, as well. Across the room, Alex was slipping out of his shirt in a manner that all but announced that his intentions didn't include anything more suggestive than retiring for the night. Alone.

Though Megan knew she ought to ignore him and go about her own bedtime routine as if the sight of a man stripping down to his skivvies were no big deal, she didn't. The fact was, she couldn't. Even as she accused herself of voyeurism, the charge couldn't compel her to avert her eyes from Alex's bare back.

Had his shoulders been that spectacular fifteen years ago? Megan didn't remember, but she was positive she wouldn't—no, *couldn't*—have forgotten something so certifiably memorable. Her fingers itched to feel the bronze skin stretched tautly over hard muscle and sinew, the same way she couldn't resist running her hands over sculpture, even when all the signs in the museums said Do Not Touch. The distinction, of course, was that Alex's skin would be warm and pliant, not cold and hard, beneath her fingertips. He also moved with a naturally fluid grace that raised the mundane act of undressing into the sublime.

By all indications oblivious to his rapt audience, Alex dropped to sit on his sleeping bag, his back toward her as he loosened the laces of his boots, tugged them off, and set them next to his pack. Once his socks were removed and tucked inside, he flexed his feet, drawing her attention away from his shoulders for an instant. It was more than enough time for her to note that his feet were long and broad and powerful looking. Right behind it followed the unbidden and thoroughly unsettling memory of the old college adage about a man's feet providing an accurate gauge for judging the measure of another, less public, appendage.

Megan was still struggling to suppress that wayward thought when Alex slowly turned to face her, his hands at his waist. Reluctantly dragging her gaze up his chest, which was golden brown beneath its triangle of tawny hair, she met his eyes, catlike, green and glimmering with reflected light.

"Something wrong?"

Neither the tone of his voice nor the expression on his face suggested the slightest awareness of what he was doing . . . or what he was doing to *her*. As he waited for an answer, he released the catch of his belt buckle in an automatic fashion.

"What are you doing?" Megan asked, sternly ordering herself to breathe at a normal rate, keep her voice even and hold her gaze fixed on his.

"Getting undressed. I can't sleep in my clothes."

Megan heard the snap give way on his jeans, then the raspy sound of the zipper being lowered, and she felt a shiver that was both anticipation and apprehension. "But—"

"For God's sake, Megan," he interrupted. "Gimme a break and don't get in an uproar over it. It's not like you've never seen a naked man before."

His thumbs hooked in the sides of his open fly, Alex peeled the jeans down his hips and, despite Megan's earlier resolve to limit her gaze to the relatively safe territory above his waist, her eyes automatically shifted downward. Though she felt her face heat, she was unable to lift her gaze again before making three unintentional but reliable observations.

Alex wasn't stripping down to his skivvies, because he still didn't wear anything but his own bare skin under jeans.

The old maxim about estimating the proportions of a man's "other" endowments based on the size of his feet wasn't a fallacy, but was based on fact. Substantial fact.

And she could stop worrying about persuading herself that she ought to defend her virtue, since Alex was *not* interested in challenging the all-too-flimsy defenses of that attribute.

"Ahem."

Megan's eyes shot back up to Alex's and her cheeks burned even more fiercely. While he didn't say a word about either her gawking or her embarrassment at getting caught in the act, words weren't necessary to convey his disdain. After pinning her gaze with his enigmatic one for a long count of three, he turned away, and slid into his sleeping bag with a slow ease that spoke volumes about his disinterest.

Rigid with fury and mortification, Megan remained where she stood for another endless moment before she was finally able to break the grip of her inertia and move. She considered taking her things and finding another, more hospitable cave in which to spend the night, but settled for unrolling her sleeping bag as far away from Alex's as she could get.

Glaring at the tousled back-of-the-head and wide shoulders that protruded from his sleeping bag, she plopped down onto her own, unlaced her boots, and yanked them off. Inevitably, the thought of clobbering him with one or both of them crossed her mind. Before she could act on the impulse, he rolled over to face her and spoke again.

"Megan?"

After making a valiant effort to control her expression and then resigning herself to the fact that it was as good as it was ever likely to get, she raised her head. "Yes?"

"You aren't going to sleep in those clothes, are you?"

The question couldn't possibly be as innocuous as it sounded—or as guileless as Alex looked, lying on his side, propped up on one elbow. Trusting her instincts more than appearances where Alex was concerned, she warily asked, "Any particular reason you want to know, or just idle curiosity?"

"No reason. Your clothes are dirty. You're sweaty."

So kind of him to mention that fact, as if she weren't aware of it already. "And?"

"Just thought you might want to keep the inside of your sleeping bag clean."

Not for a second did she believe the question was motivated by concern for her comfort and well-being. Though she couldn't put her finger on a reason for the sensation, she felt as if she were being backed into a corner, and there was nothing she could do or say to prevent it from happening.

"Suffering from a sudden attack of modesty?"

Suffering from a sudden certainty that the corner was inches away from her back and getting closer with every breath was more like it.

"Don't worry about it, Megan. It's not like I haven't seen a naked woman before."

That remark hemmed her in, until she could almost feel the hard surface of the walls against her shoulder blades.

"It's not like I haven't seen *you* naked before."

She was trapped. Like her own earlier "Chicken," it was a challenge. She wouldn't be able to ignore it, any more than he'd been able to. As far as she could tell, the only way out of this was to kill him.

His jaw propped on one loose fist, his eyes hooded so she couldn't see them, Alex waited.

Megan reminded herself that murder was illegal, even in now anarchistic Zoman. And if the Zomanis didn't catch and punish her for it, Alex's employers would undoubtedly make up for that oversight. Both prospects were equally gruesome, given their vast respective experience in such matters, and no connections she had in either quarter would save her. Left with no other choice, she took a deep breath and began to unbutton her shirt.

Stone-faced and unmoving, like a horizontal wooden cigar-store Indian, Alex watched and waited.

Seven buttons later, Megan slipped off the shirt and laid it atop her backpack. Grimly determined to get through with this as quickly and painlessly as possible, she stood, undid the button at her waist, and slid down the tab of the zipper. Loose as they were, her shorts dropped to the floor, leaving her clad in only a bra and panties. She faltered, holding her breath as she waited for Alex to make the next move, to beckon her nearer, to . . .

"See you in the morning, Megan. G'night." With a tired—*bored?*—yawn, Alex rolled over, pulled the edge of the sleeping bag over his shoulders, and settled in for the night.

That did it. First, she was going to kill him, and then she was burning the underwear. Plain white cotton and as functional as a garment could get, it was far too modest to be titillating to any but the most desperate of men. If she wore it on a stroll through a prison yard— or perhaps in downtown Tel Mapur, that most orthodox of Middle Eastern cities—chances were slightly better than even that someone might take a second look.

*Obviously, Alex isn't that desperate,* Megan thought as she quickly shed the rest of her clothing and burrowed into her sleeping bag. *He isn't even interested— in either the underwear or me.*

He'd made that point as clear as it could get, which was a lot clearer than it had really needed to be. It hurt a lot more than it should have, too. Although crawling into bed with Alex again was the very last thing she'd intended to do, it would have seemed more like a conscious decision and less like default if she could have been the refuser instead of the refused.

*And Alex had known that.*

The thought made Megan squirm, even as she reminded herself that she'd known there was bound to be some sort of reprisal for her earlier "Chicken." She didn't know what she'd expected, but it certainly hadn't been that Alex would raise the stakes of the challenge so high, turning what should have been a simple—even petty—little retaliation into a full-scale, no-holds-barred act of vengeance.

He had, though. She would have seen it coming, too, if she hadn't let herself get so sidetracked by false hopes and hormones. Rubbing her nose in the fact that he could tell she still wanted him as much as she had fifteen years before would have vindicated her "Chicken" effectively enough, but going on to *show* her that he didn't want her was indisputably overkill. If he always approached his job with such ruthless efficiency, it was no wonder Alex was the Agency's favorite son.

As far as Megan was concerned, however, Alex was absolutely despicable. With that little effort, he'd dredged up a host of old insecurities she'd thought had been confronted and conquered a long time ago. Like the unwelcome ghost from her past that had walked over the hill and into her life again that afternoon, they had all returned—the doubts, the feelings of inadequacy, even the unbearable resignation to the fact that she was undesirable, which had plagued her when she'd first met Alex. The old feelings infuriated her almost as much as he did.

And never mind the fact that they'd been the real reason she'd seduced Alex Sullivan in the first place.

IT HAD BEEN SPRING break in Fort Lauderdale, everything *Where the Boys Are* had promised, though the swimsuits had been a lot skimpier and Connie Francis hadn't been anywhere in sight. There had been hundreds—no, *thousands*—of students on the beach, the sweet-and-sour smells of cocoa butter, pot, and beer in the air, and the din of radios and tape players competing in a battle of musical styles that had rock, disco, and country and western all struggling for dominance.

Megan had never intended to be there—at least not that year—but her friend Rita, who *had* planned to come, had been diagnosed with mono two weeks before. Since Rita had already paid her share of the expenses and the others couldn't afford to give back her money, Megan had wheedled it out of her father and come in her place. At that point, she had been there six hours, most of which she'd spent trying to decide whether or not she'd made a big mistake. . . .

Since the other girls were Rita's friends from high school and freshman students at Temple, not Muhlenberg, where she and Rita went to school, Megan didn't know them any better than a person *could* know five virtual strangers with whom one had just spent twenty-four hours in a car. Despite the fact that they'd only booked one room, it didn't look as if she was going to get to know them much better, either.

The L'Oréal twins, who weren't really twins except in their preference of hair color, had never meant to spend their vacation with the others; their boyfriends, Sigma Chis from Georgetown, had snagged somebody's father's condo over in Boca Raton. Wendy, an undeclared premed who was all but failing chemistry, had come to the beach with her, but was thoroughly immersed in the wonderful world of double and covalent bonding. That left Courtney and Jennifer, who were both so gorgeous, they could have been poster girls for Florida tourism, a fact that had not gone unnoticed by any conscious male in Broward County, as far as she could tell.

On the whole, it looked like it was going to be a very long week. Possibly interminable. If Megan didn't die of boredom, she was going to get trampled by the hordes around her.

While there didn't seem to be much she could do about the first of those fates, the second was avoidable, with a solution as simple as removing herself from the crowd. After rising to her feet and tugging her functional, if unstylish, turquoise maillot down in back, she headed off toward the concession stand. Once she'd picked her way through the sandy maze of beach blankets and prone bodies, she found a line so long, she felt she might get to the head of it sometime around Memorial Day. Much sooner than that, she met Alex Sullivan.

It was his voice that got to her first. Deep and low, with a drawl as thick and rich as Texas crude, she wouldn't have cared what he said, as long as she could listen to him speak. "Hi."

Though Megan was sure he had to be talking to somebody else, her eyes shot up to his, which were fixed on her. In addition to being far enough above hers that she had to tip back her head to look into them, they were the most beautiful green she'd ever seen, like clear, flawless emeralds. Her heart skipped a beat as she panicked and thought about making a hasty, if cowardly, retreat; but then she pulled herself together, summoned up her best sultry look, and smiled.

"Hi, yourself." Tilting her head to one side, she crossed her arms over her midriff. As early as thirteen, she'd observed that that particular pose pushed up her breasts, giving the illusion of cleavage. "Is there some kind of height requirement down there in Texas? Legal minimum of six feet?"

"We kill off the runts in junior high," he told her dryly, apparently getting the joke and appreciating it. "Either that or ship 'em up north, where it doesn't matter so much. I wouldn't think *you'd* complain about it."

"It wasn't a complaint, just an observation." She tightened her arms slightly and was gratified to note that his gaze drifted to the modestly scooped neckline of her suit. Apparently, he *saw* something he appreciated, too. "Maybe I should move there."

"No tall men back in . . . ?"

"Pennsylvania," Megan provided with a smile and a shake of her head. "Pitifully few."

"I told you that's where we sent the few we let live." His grin gave her trouble swallowing, and she wasn't doing any better breathing. She told herself not to worry about it, because it was a good sign. The best, actually. "I'm Alex Sullivan, U.T.—that's Texas, just in case you had any doubts about it—junior, poli sci."

After a moment's hesitation, Megan answered.

"Eden Franklin..."

She nearly choked on the lie, but forced herself to go on.

"Temple..."

The second lie came a little easier.

"Freshman, art history and anthropology."

There was no point in making this any more complicated than it had to be; as it was, she was already skating on terrifyingly thin ice.

It could get a lot thinner. Within the hour, Megan and Alex were in his roommate's battered VW Bug, on their way to a beach he'd heard was less of a mob scene. As it turned out, that was particularly true that afternoon with the arrival of a tropical storm that tested the rule that March was too early in the season for hurricanes. Because the car's windshield wipers dated back to the first Nixon administration, they had no choice but to sit out the downpour in the beach's deserted parking lot.

The first twenty minutes seemed interminable, but not due to boredom. Megan was edgy with tension and apprehension, inundated with second thoughts—and then third ones—about what she was doing there. Mostly, they were doubts. Though Alex had spirited her off to this isolated location, she couldn't help wondering if he'd ever really intended for them to have this much privacy.

Certainly, nothing he'd done since their arrival suggested he had. A little small talk, a shared beer he'd appropriated, along with the car keys, from his roommate, and a great deal of peering out at the vast gray

expanse of the Atlantic through the steamy windshield
and driving rain could pretty much summarize his
contribution to the festivities. Not by so much as a
touch of his hand or a meaningful glance had he hinted
at any ulterior motive.

*Damn.* At this rate, she was never going to lose her
virginity, unless she went completely off the deep end,
resigned herself to looking like the worst kind of slut,
and jumped him.

"Eden?"

The delay before Megan responded was only due in
part to her distracted efforts to find some other, less
vulgar way to ravish Alex; lamentably, most of it was
because it had slipped her mind that "Eden" was supposed to be her name. Her gaze flew up, and she prayed
she didn't look as startled and guilty as she felt.

"Yes, Alex?" she finally said, her voice sounding
slightly strangled, even to her own ears.

If Alex noticed anything odd about either her voice
or her behavior, he kept that observation to himself.
His expression church-solemn, he quietly asked, "Can
I kiss you?"

Her heart leaped up into her throat, rendering her
incapable of speech.

"Can I, Eden?"

A shiver scurried through her body, unrelated to the
swift drop in temperature that had come with the
storm. The one thing she wasn't was cold. Heat rose
within her like a fever, making her lick her lips reflexively before she gulped and gave him an unsteady nod.
"Yes."

He smiled, his look of pleased confidence suggesting
she'd already agreed to much more than a kiss. While

it epitomized centuries of masculine presumption, she didn't hold that against him. Under the circumstances, the last thing she wanted was a man who'd been so thoroughly enlightened by modern thinking that he believed he ought to respect her. Respect was good, most of the time, but there were occasions when *lust* was a lot better. This was one of them.

Megan felt its force—and Alex's deliberate restraint of it—as he leaned across the console that separated their seats, cupped one hand behind her nape, and gently drew her toward him. Though his mouth scarcely brushed hers in that first feather-light caress, there was nothing tentative about it. Even in her limited experience, which amounted to a couple of unpleasant incidents provoked by frat rats who'd been as drunk as they were determined to avail themselves of any warm, semiwilling female body, she recognized that Alex knew enough about kissing for both of them. She'd always been a quick learner. It seemed like a combination with all the earmarks of destiny.

Within a couple of moments, however, Megan was forced to acknowledge that the situation might also have all the potential for disaster. She'd never suspected so many awkward mechanics were involved in kissing, and following Alex's lead didn't quite cover everything. There was that little—but vital—detail about tilting her head in the opposite direction so their noses wouldn't collide. And the problem of when, exactly, she ought to open her mouth. And the matter of what to do with her hands. For the time being, she kept them in her lap.

"So sweet . . ."

When he groaned against her mouth, the soft sound of arousal felt like praise, assuring her she must be doing something right. Encouraged, Megan began to relax and then, as her anxiety ebbed, to enjoy his touch enough to feel tension of a completely different variety. Her nerves tingled as the caress of his fingers on the back of her neck, the flick of his tongue on her bottom lip, and the touch of his hand on her bare thigh all sent tiny electric vibrations skittering through her. As they converged in the most feminine part of her, they generated a reaction that was so spontaneous and overwhelming, it had to be primal in origin.

Instincts she hadn't known she possessed transcended the limitations of innocence. Her upper body strained toward his, rubbing her breasts against his chest. The motion scuffed the thin cotton and nylon of their clothing together, generating a friction that peaked her nipples into hard little buds. When she gasped at the sensation, his tongue followed the breath as it flowed into her mouth. It was a hot, moist invasion she welcomed eagerly as he found the most sensitive regions of her mouth and paid homage to them. With a purr of exquisite pleasure, she lifted her hands to his shoulders, clinging to what was rapidly becoming the only stable fixture in her increasingly tumultuous world. Never mind that *he* was causing all the turmoil.

"Alex . . ." She sighed, her voice and body trembling as his hand slid slowly but surely over her hip and up her torso. The sleek fabric of her swimsuit acted more like a conductor than a buffer when his palm grazed the underside of her breast and his thumb stroked across her nipple; she quivered as if she'd just touched a live wire.

"So responsive..." she heard him murmur against the pulse point below her ear. His mouth nuzzled the spot as he began to describe, in lavishly explicit terms, the things he envisioned doing with her. His suggestions might have been obscene if they hadn't been so exciting. "It'll be so good, darlin'..."

Megan shuddered with anticipation as her eyes drifted shut and her head lolled back against the strong support of his hand. Through the haze of passion and drawled promises came the raspy voice of Rod Stewart, belting out "Tonight's the Night" as if he were singing just for them. "Oh, God..."

"Eden, darlin', do you have any idea how much I want you?"

With his heart beating convincingly against her palm, Megan supposed she did. Still, hearing Alex say the words was far more compelling than she could ever have imagined... even if the name he spoke wasn't really hers. Nodding and hoping he wouldn't see the lie reflected there, she opened her eyes and looked directly into his.

There was no sign of doubt in those gleaming green eyes—just blatant masculine appreciation and an arousal so potent, she couldn't help but feel a rush of feminine pride in having inspired them. His hand moved to his own chest and covered hers. "Do you?"

"Do I what?" she whispered.

"Know how much I want you?" he repeated softly, lowering his hand to his groin and taking hers, very willingly, with it. When he laid her hand over the front of his swim trunks, the proud swell of his manhood surged against her palm. "This much, darlin'."

As if acting of their own volition, Megan's fingers traced the length of his erection and then curled around it. Impressed, and at the same time a bit intimidated, by what she found, she swallowed heavily.

So did he. His voice sounding strangely congested, Alex asked, "Do you want this, darlin'? Are you sure?"

"Yes," she breathed, nodding.

He smiled. "Can you imagine how it'll be, Eden? Me, deep inside you, and . . ."

Reacting involuntarily to the sensuality of his words, her fingers tightened. Groaning, Alex moved her hand down onto his bare thigh. "Not yet, darlin', and not here, for God's sake."

Megan flushed, more embarrassed at forgetting they were in a car than by the intimate manner in which she'd been caressing him. Her fingers itched to do it again, and rubbed against the rough surface of his leg with the reaction.

"In case you haven't noticed, neither one of us is exactly built for doing it in a Volkswagen. We're both way too long for that." His gaze roved down her legs, appraising their length. She felt the touch as if the contact were physical, and liked it. It made her feel more desirable than she'd ever felt in her life—infinitely so, as if her inordinate height had suddenly become a blessing, rather than a misfortune.

"And," he continued, his drawl mesmerizing her, "in case you haven't noticed it, a quickie isn't what I had in mind. I don't think that's what you want, either."

She shook her head. In some remote, still-sentient recess of her mind, Megan wondered if the reason she'd found his drawl so fascinating was that she'd secretly speculated he made love in the same slow, languorous manner in which he talked.

"And, in case you haven't noticed, it's stopped raining. I don't have the slightest doubt that this parking lot's gonna get awful crowded mighty fast when a couple thousand people realize they can come back to the beach. I don't mind a little kinkiness now and then— just mild stuff and for the sake of variety, you understand—but I think these things oughta be confined to two people, without an audience."

Megan lifted her head to look out through the windshield, and she saw that Alex was right. It had stopped raining. The sun was out, as bright as before the storm, rapidly evaporating the few scattered puddles still remaining on the asphalt. A few cars had already pulled back into the lot, and she could see people, mostly students, walking toward the beach. Turning back to Alex, Megan smiled and moved her hand suggestively on his thigh. "Two's exactly what I had in mind."

"Well, then—" Alex leaned across the gearshift to press a quick, hard kiss on her mouth "—Eden, darlin', what do you say we head on back to the hotel?"

ACROSS THE CAVE FROM Megan, Alex shifted restlessly within the confines of his sleeping bag, in defiance of his own mental orders to stop all the fidgeting and get to sleep. He couldn't. Hadn't been able to for hours. And being in a cave had little or nothing to do with his difficulty. It just went to show that a man could get used to anything, if he set his mind to it . . . or if some even more disturbing problem came along to eclipse it.

*Megan.*

Now, *there* was one long, blond problem that could drive a man to the brink of insanity. Beyond it, if that senseless stunt he'd pulled earlier was any indication.

Three hours later, he was still trying to figure out where his mind had been at the time. He'd never imagined stripping down to the bare skin in front of Megan would turn out to be such an erotic experience—an oversight that could only be accounted for if his brain had gone AWOL again. On a *real* mission, that kind of error might have cost him his life.

As it was, the consequences of his miscalculation were dire enough. In his effort to prove that Megan's wiles weren't going to distract him this time around, he'd come *this* far from proving just the opposite, to be spared only by the cover of his sleeping bag. It was a good thing scientists hadn't figured out a way to make those space-age polymers any thinner, because he'd needed every millimeter of bulk he could get, especially once Megan had begun to undress. Turning away hadn't kept him from hearing her moving around, and it had taken the last traces of his self-control not to peek. At that point, there hadn't been much left, either; it had taken a lot to restrain the urge to crawl across the floor and beg.

His self-control hadn't been able to do anything about his imagination. Primed to go during the flight, it had been lunging along ever since he'd seen her when he'd stepped over the top of the hill. Still was, for that matter, making him hard and hot and *very* bothered— with the simultaneous cause and cure of his malady both within the range of his touch and totally out of reach. And, while Megan *ought* to be squirming as much as he was, she was asleep.

As Alex stared at the back of her head, the light from the lantern gleamed on the golden cap of her hair. He wanted to touch it, feel its silky warmth against his fingertips, bury his face in it and smell the rich, potent scent that was so thoroughly imbued in his memory that, even now, the most evanescent wisps of that fragrance were perceptible. Its subtle impact hit him hard, but then the sleeping bag slid off her shoulder, revealing smooth ivory skin and the fact that she *couldn't* be wearing anything beneath the cover, except, at most, the band-legged panties that had made him think she wasn't wearing any under her shorts.

And *that* was the last thing he needed to think about at this particular moment. Instead, he ought to remember the ways she'd lied to, manipulated, and aggravated him. She was the only woman he'd ever known who could make him blindingly livid, dumb as a fence post, and hard as one, all at the same time.

Damn woman.

He didn't understand it—not his desire for Megan, which was evident enough, but everything else. Her lies. Her manipulations. The way she went out of her way to aggravate him, when she wanted him, too. He'd seen it in her eyes, though she'd done her best to conceal it. Trying to lure it out of her had been the only thing that had kept him undressing long after he should have had the good sense to stop. What she'd revealed had been so much like the desire he'd seen in her eyes so long ago in Florida.

# 5

THEY'D BARELY MADE IT back to the hotel room after Alex saw the Emergency Stop button in the elevator and began wondering if he might be entitled to his own interpretation of exactly what constituted an actual emergency. Only two things had kept him from pushing it: his certainty that it was wired to a central alarm, and his desire to behold the full length of her sprawled out on a bed. It was the second, beyond question, that had actually convinced him.

Lord, Eden was tall, and a substantial portion of that length was legs. He'd always been a leg man, too. They'd been the first thing he'd noticed, setting her apart from the thousands of other women on the beach. Though his roommate and fraternity brother, Andy, a devoted breast man, had said she was flat-chested, Alex had thought she was sleek; big breasts on that long, lean body would have been as incongruous as antlers on a duck.

Size didn't matter anyway, especially when breasts were as sensitive as hers, making her shiver with visible arousal when he touched her. Seeing that shiver had made him want to touch her again. It had made him want a lot more . . . and unless something went dreadfully, horribly wrong in the next couple of minutes, he was going to have every one of those wants fulfilled.

That thought made his breath quicken with anticipation as he shut the door to his hotel room and switched on the light. A quick glance established that his bag was the only one remaining. Following the unwritten but nonetheless binding code of fraternity living, Andy, L.C. and Bubba had all vacated the premises. He made a mental note that he owed them each a jug from that old bootlegger over in Denton when they got back to school, then turned back to Eden.

She was standing beside the door, fidgeting with the strap of her handbag and staring at the bed with eyes huge as saucers. It confirmed his earlier impression that she didn't make a habit of this, and he offered up a silent word of thanks to whatever forces were responsible for designating him an exception. The inference that she'd simply been overwhelmed by desire for him was too tempting to resist.

So was she. Smoothly and suddenly—the transition made him wonder if he'd only imagined her hesitancy—she dropped her handbag, leaned back against the door, and met his gaze directly with a come-hither look that hit him with the same impact as a sip of straight moonshine.

He came, closing the distance between them and lifting his hands to grip the sides of her head. He claimed her mouth, and she welcomed him eagerly, her lips parted and her arms raised for his embrace. As his body settled against hers, he couldn't help but marvel at how perfectly they fit, even upright. Unlike the shorter women he'd known, which was, not surprisingly, the vast majority of them, her hips were level with his, as were her breasts and his chest, and her mouth was only slightly lower than his own. Neither had to strain as they deepened the kiss and he pressed her back against the door, grinding his hips against hers. He ached, not just *there*, but everywhere.

As if she did, too, she wriggled against him and whimpered, the sound vibrating across his tongue. He groaned as he felt her leg slide up the outside of his own. The skin on the inside of her thigh was soft and silky against his hair-roughened leg; the heat that radiated from the place where it joined her body was so intense, it penetrated the fabric of their bathing suits to curl around him like a warm fist. He rubbed against her, growling in frustration at the barrier.

"Darlin' . . ." he whispered against the delicate shell of her ear. "Can we get rid of this?"

"This" was her swimsuit, indicated by the narrow strap under which he hooked his fingers, brushing them over the smooth upper curve of her breast.

She smiled, opening her eyes. As he'd noted the first time he'd seen them, they were as blue as the Atlantic Ocean had been that day. Now, however, they were burning with an inner fire that heated his blood to boiling. "Yes."

Short as the word was, even before it was finished, her hand moved up toward her shoulder. He stopped it before it got there. "*I* want to do it. If you'd like to return the favor and undress *me* when I'm through . . ."

His voice caught in his throat as she smiled again at the suggestion. With a look of pure, deliberate provocation, she rode her fingertip along the waistband of his trunks and purred, "Do I have to wait?"

"Yes," Alex hissed, catching her hand just as she found the drawstring and threatened to pull it loose. He was still holding her hand when they tumbled onto the bed, rolling over and over in a flurry of kisses and caresses.

When it ended, he was *still* holding her hand. Both of her hands, actually, stretched up over her head as she lay flat on her back beneath him. While he could have straddled her hips and pinned her down a lot sooner, he'd been enjoying the tussle too much to end it. It looked as if she'd enjoyed it, too.

With all that blond hair fanned out around her head in a disorderly halo, she resembled a fallen angel. Her face was flushed, her eyes glistening. Her lips, kiss-swollen and dewy, parted as she dragged in a deep breath, a movement that drew his eyes down to her chest. Beneath the thin nylon of her bathing suit, her nipples stood out prominently, as if in invitation. Lowering his head, he flicked his tongue over one and felt it pucker more tightly. He captured the hard peak between his lips, teasing it with his teeth and then soothing it with his tongue until she writhed beneath him, tossing her head from side to side and making small whimpering sounds of wordless demand.

Knowing what she wanted and wanting it, too, he released her hands, rocked back onto his heels, and reached for the straps of her bathing suit. As she lowered her arms so he could slide them off her shoulders, her hands came to rest on his thighs, making him pause.

"Please, Alex . . ." she murmured, opening her eyes to gaze up at him with a frank desire that was more arousing than anything he'd ever known. It held that distinction for less than a second until she bent her knee, pressing her thigh against the base of his scrotum and moving it slightly. That tiny movement was more than arousing; it blew him away.

"My God, Eden..." he moaned as he leaned forward to kiss her with swift, hard urgency. While he'd intended to take his time, lingering over every part of her body and letting her do the same to him, the evidence that *she* couldn't wait consigned his own patience to oblivion. He wanted her, and he wanted her *now.*

Backing off the bed, he peeled the clingy fabric of her suit off her body. Before it hit the floor, his T-shirt was on its way over his head and she'd pulled loose the knot in the drawstring of his swim trunks. They puddled around his feet and he kicked them aside before crawling back onto the bed ... and onto Eden.

"Oh, God, darlin'," he muttered, his mouth against her collarbone. The trace of saltiness on his tongue prompted him to reflect, for an instant, that she'd been in the ocean once during her vacation; equally fleeting was the notion inspired by the scent of tanning lotion, that at least she'd seen the sun. If he had anything to say about it, she'd go back to Pennsylvania as pale as she'd come, and the only salt water she'd encounter between now and then was that of their perspiration.

"Alex..." When she said his name, it sounded like a prayer, and her body arched up toward his in supplication. He slid his hand down her ribs, over her hip, and between her legs to verify that she was as ready as she seemed.

She was. Creamy against his fingers, her body quivered at that slight touch, as if she would come the instant he entered her. The way he felt, he wouldn't be far behind. While, as a woman, she was fortunate enough to have more than one climax in her, he was only a man, and he'd be done, at least for the time being, if that happened. As he claimed her mouth and poised himself over her, he tried to delay that conclusion by focusing on something other than her legs wrapped around his hips, her hands clutching his shoulders, and, most crucially, how good it was going to feel once he was inside her.

There it was. Music somewhere down the hall... "Feels Like The First Time." He ordered himself to ignore the driving rhythm and concentrate, instead, on Foreigner's elaborate harmonies.

The music was completely forgotten, however, as he sank into her and they both cried out—him with shock and her, he was sure, in pain. It didn't just feel like the first time; as he discovered, it *was*—for her, anyway.

Careful not to move his hips, he pulled his head back far enough to see her face, gaped down at her, and choked, "Oh, Lord, darlin'..."

She opened her eyes, tears glimmering in them as she assured him, "It's okay, Alex. I'm all right."

She was lying through her teeth, which were gritted tightly together. As if that sign wasn't obvious enough, he could see it in her eyes, hear it in her voice, feel it in the unmistakably *non*sexual tension in her body. Holding his lower body motionless and forcing himself to ignore its insistently throbbing demand, he quietly said, "No extra credits for bravery now, darlin'. Is there something you forgot to tell me?"

More tears welled in her eyes. He got the feeling they weren't from physical pain, but didn't understand why, exactly. Raising his hand and stroking his fingers across the pink-flushed skin of her cheek, he told her, "It'll be okay, darlin', as soon as you relax. The tough part's over now."

In a constricted voice, she admitted, "I'm certainly glad to hear that."

He smiled as he lowered his mouth to hers, gently coaxing her to open it for him as she had earlier. Though she responded slowly at first, he felt her apprehension gradually dwindling as she again surrendered to passion. By the time her heels dug into his buttocks and her hips shifted restlessly beneath his, he was more than willing to proceed. "There now, darlin'... Isn't that better?" he whispered against her mouth as he moved inside her tight feminine sheath for the first time.

With a small, wordless cry, she averred that he was right.

"And, darlin', hold on, 'cause it's gonna get better yet."

It did. Determined to make up for the initial pain, Alex set about the enjoyable task of giving her every kind of pleasure a man could possibly offer a woman. Though he took infinite delight in the giving, she returned his caresses with such sweet enthusiasm, it overwhelmed him. As did her cry of blissful amazement when her first climax engulfed her.

Her second, too...moments later, when he was also consumed by her fire. And as they both went up in flames, the last thing he remembered was calling her name.

"Alex?"

Though, as an Agency-conditioned habit, Alex usually woke instantly, clear as a bell and ready for action, his inadequate, dream-plagued sleep had left him addled and cloudy, past and present muddling together, as indistinguishable as if they were one and the same.

"Alex?" repeated the feminine whisper that had taunted him throughout the night; simultaneously, satiny fingertips that had known every inch of his body prodded at his bare shoulder.

*Again?* he thought fuzzily, though his body responded with remarkable speed and force. Blood surged into his groin, and his entire body ached with arousal. At this rate, she was going to kill him, but at least he'd go happy.

His eyes still shut, he lifted his hand, cupped the back of her head, and pulled her down until her mouth brushed across his. Her lips were soft and warm and moist, tasting of cinnamon and passion. He didn't just want to touch her, kiss her, possess her—he *had* to do all of those things, and it went way beyond mere desire, becoming a genuine need.

Arching his neck and lifting his head from the floor, Alex strained for greater contact, though at first he didn't get it. Tensing the muscles in his arm, he drew her back toward him until her lips met his again, and he slipped his free arm around her waist, pulling her down on top of him.

Though she'd spent a large part of the night cataloging the thousands of reasons she shouldn't still be attracted to Alex, at that moment, Megan couldn't summon the will to invoke a single one of them. All Alex had to do was touch her, and her response sent them scurrying into insignificance.

Murmuring his name in a breathless sigh, she entangled her fingers in the lush thickness of his hair and covered his mouth with hers. His lips parted in invitation, and she plunged her tongue eagerly into the depths of his mouth. Her senses reeled, inundated with the sound of his groan, the scent of his skin, the incomparable wet heat of his mouth, and the odd sensation of erotic power that welled up within her at her own show of aggression and his approval of it.

Her head was still spinning when he pushed her back onto the soft cushion of the sleeping bag and slid over her. His lips captured hers as his hands roved up and down her body, finding the buttons of her shirt and working them loose. They skimmed her midriff, the contrast of gentle touch and rough texture making her shiver, and then his fingertips edged under the band of her bra. He kissed her again, his tongue probing deeply into her mouth as his fingers stole up toward her nipple. It contracted even before he touched it; when he did, she threw back her head, whimpered, and called out his name.

"It's been so long, darlin'," he whispered against the side of her throat. "And, God, you're so beautiful. I want you so much, Eden, I can—"

His declaration was cut off abruptly by the sudden furious thrashing of her body beneath his. She wasn't struggling to get the cover out from between them, as Alex believed at first, for an all-too-brief, promising moment, but instead was fighting to get his weight off her. He was so dazed, it took him a moment to figure out what had prompted her change of mind, until his words replayed in his head and he realized what he'd said. He'd called her *Eden*. A chill washing over him, he released her and sat up.

Megan sat up, too. Trembling violently, she pulled her shirt closed. Her head was bowed, her legs pulled in tightly, as if she were trying to withdraw all five feet, eleven and three-quarters inches of her inside the shirt and disappear. Again.

And Alex would be damned if he'd let her do it. This time around, he could see it coming, and he intended to head it off before she got a running start. "Megan, I'm sorry. I don't know why I said . . ."

"Dammit, Alex," she breathed, her chest heaving and her eyes glistening with tears. Whether they were angry or anguished, he wasn't sure. "I won't let you do this to me. Not again."

It sounded too much like what he'd been thinking himself, though he was sure it was for an entirely different reason—one he didn't understand.

"Correct me if I'm wrong," he began, his low growl of frustration checked at that volume only through strenuous effort, "but right up until I called you Eden, you were kissing me back. Don't deny it, Megan. You wanted me."

Color rushed into her face, as good as an admission, but he pressed her for a real answer. "Didn't you, Megan?"

"For God's sake, Alex," she snapped. "Not for revenge."

"Revenge?" Alex echoed blankly, recalling his dumb little retaliation the night before and wondering what that had to do with it. As far as he could tell, the only thing the two had in common was that they had ended up naked—or nearly so—twice, with both of them thoroughly aroused and not a chance in hell of any relief for it. "Revenge for what, Megan?"

She gulped visibly. "For Florida."

Alex stared at her, speechless. Why would she think he'd want revenge for what had happened between them in Florida? It had been one of the most incredibly beautiful experiences of his life, even if it had also been one of the most utterly baffling. He had to know. "Megan, what happened in Florida?"

The blood drained from her face as quickly as it had come in and she choked, "We had an affair...."

He knew that part; in fact, it was the only thing he'd ever been sure about. "But, Megan...what *really* happened?"

Her gaze skittered away, eluding his, and her voice was barely audible. Her words, however, slammed into him like the blast of an explosion. "I heard the guys on spring break just wanted to get a tan, get drunk, and get—"

Alex's hand whipped out to grasp her jaw, and he turned her face back toward his, demanding, "You went to Florida intending to get laid?"

"Not *intending*," she protested. "Just *prepared*. I went to the doctor and ..."

His oath, while soft, encompassed a great deal of expressive territory. "Megan..."

"Dammit, Alex, I was only nineteen," she argued defensively. "I was a kid, I was stupid.... I'm sorry, okay?"

*Sorry?* There were a great many things he wanted her to be, and sorry wasn't one of them. He wished he could take the whole situation back to before he'd called her Eden. For that matter, he wished he could take it all the way back to Florida. While neither objective was logical, he wasn't thinking with his brain at that moment; the regions below his waist had staged a coup . . . and were winning.

And she thought it was *revenge*? Against whom? Himself?

"Dammit, Megan . . ." In a crude but effective demonstration of his own misery, his hand snaked out, encircled her wrist, and yanked her hand beneath the cover of the sleeping bag. Pressing it against him where he hurt most, he forced her fingers to wrap around him. "What does that feel like to you?"

*Hard. Smooth. Hot.* It throbbed in her hand and a warm, wet bead dripped onto her wrist. Megan swallowed heavily at the same instant her fingers clenched of their own accord.

Alex made a choked little noise, but held her hand where it was. "I was like this the whole time we were in Florida. I've been like this since I walked over the hill and saw you yesterday afternoon. And I'm damn sure it's not revenge!"

A memory flashed into Megan's mind, vivid as a photograph. "But, last night, when you took off your jeans . . ."

"Control, Megan," he said in a cold, tight voice. "Pure self-control. And I paid for it for hours, too. While you fell asleep, I lay awake half the night . . ."

This time, *she* made a choked little noise and snatched back her hand. "What'd you expect, Alex? For me to crawl into that sleeping bag with you and take care of it?"

"Don't tell me you didn't think about it, because I won't believe you."

As Megan glared at him, words she'd heard someone say back in college suddenly came out of her mouth, before her brain even knew they were there. "Any warm body is preferable to your own right hand?"

After glowering silently at her for a moment, Alex grabbed his flashlight, levered himself to his feet, and strode to the back of the room. As he arrived at the passage leading to the bathroom, he turned back to her, naked and seemingly unaware of that fact. "No, Megan, any warm body is *not* preferable."

As shocked at his rejection as if he'd slapped her, Megan stared after Alex for several minutes after he was out of sight. At last she cursed under her breath, far angrier with herself than with him. She'd been the one who'd been wide-awake, the one who should have called a halt to it—and long before she'd found herself on her back, checking out the cave's ceiling.

What was she, anyway—an absolute idiot?

The only way this scene could have been any more humiliating was if she'd spilled her guts and admitted the truth: that she'd been a pathetic wretch, all arms and legs and rampant insecurity, when she'd met Alex in Fort Lauderdale. She'd always been able to take some small comfort in thinking she'd hidden it from him, but that demonstration last night—and the one this morning—hinted he'd known all along.

She'd been the last virgin left. Maybe not on the planet, but certainly on her freshman floor. She'd actually started to worry about being the last surviving virgin in North America. While the conclusion might have seemed a trifle premature a few weeks past her nineteenth birthday, she'd already attained the dubious public distinction of being the only woman on her floor who hadn't been out on a date since their arrival in September. For that matter, though no one at school had been aware of the embarrassing truth and she would never have confessed it, at that point she'd never been on a date in her life.

If her lack of social life and its resultant celibacy could have been attributed to moral convictions or a strict upbringing, it would have been different; both, however, could be ascribed to the fact that she'd reached her full height in eighth grade and the rest of her development had waited years to catch up with it. All through high school, she'd felt like a freak, taller than most of the boys and horribly aware that her height, which hadn't even been ameliorated by a single feminine curve, was the main thing that kept them from noticing her.

She'd been repeatedly assured that everything would change once she got to college. Her mother, who, if tall, had been both beautiful and curvaceous, had told her that guys grew later and would surpass her in height as they approached adulthood. Her father, an NCAA All-Star, had sworn with equal conviction that maturity would make them aware there were more important things than a girl's height. She'd been naive enough to believe them, until she'd gotten to college and found that things were pretty much the same. She still didn't date . . . or anything else.

Though the guys in college were older and taller, they still weren't particularly interested in dating a tall, gangly female when shorter, prettier, more voluptuous and more desirable women were available. Sex was another issue altogether—the exception that proved the rule. When it came to sex, no interested woman was too tall, too homely, too unattractive, or too undesirable to stand ignored on the sidelines for long—not even her.

She'd been interested enough to contemplate not holding out for the elusive Mr. Right, a man whose existence she'd genuinely doubted, but not nearly enough to overlook the reality that the liberated sexual milieu of the late seventies wasn't quite the utopia it was purported to be. Utopia didn't take into account the awkwardness of a morning—or a life—afterward. She'd quickly learned all about that, albeit secondhand.

It had been a small school. And, just like in a small town, everybody knew everything, no matter how intimate. If the woman wasn't actually dating the guy she finally did it with, if it turned out to be nothing more than a one-night stand, she couldn't avoid seeing him—and all his friends, who undoubtedly knew the last grisly details—every day, knowing that he—and they—remembered everything. One girl she'd known had even *transferred* to another school, where people didn't know her story.

It had been early in their second term when one appallingly sordid story had prompted Rita to suggest to Megan that it might be better if the first time was with a total stranger, someone she *knew* she'd never see again, so that nothing like that could happen to her. Although Rita had been well beyond half-drunk at the time—they'd been sampling a bottle of sloe gin a senior on Megan's floor had bought for them—she'd known what she was saying and meant it, too. And even though Megan had been just as loaded when she'd agreed, she'd known exactly what *she* was saying, and meant it, too.

Then she'd gone to Florida on spring break, taken one look at Alex Sullivan, and decided *he* was the total stranger she'd had in mind. She'd been naive enough to imagine it would be easy to go back to school afterward, with her virginity left behind and her heart and dignity intact. No false expectations, no waiting for phone calls that never came, no gossip, no embarrassment.

She'd been wrong.

It wasn't that simple, she'd quickly realized, soon after her return to school. No amount of gossip or embarrassment could possibly be as bad as missing Alex, who'd become a lot more than a convenient means to an end. Though she'd been miserable, she couldn't do a thing about it. Since she'd lied to him about her name, her school, and virtually everything else, he couldn't contact her, and neither her self-respect nor her common sense would let her pick up the phone, give him a casual call, and say, "Oh, by the way. . ." During their week together, Alex had never given her a clue about how such a call would be received; even then, long before the Agency had gotten hold of him, he'd been nearly as remote and inaccessible as a Severe-Style sculpture. While he'd been, even judging by her limited experience, hell on wheels in bed, he hadn't appeared to have a clue how to relate to another human being outside that realm.

Like an idiot, she'd seen it as a challenge. She'd spent the biggest part of the week trying to prove she could unearth the feelings she was convinced *had* to be hidden beneath all that unyielding stoicism. Just often enough to be encouraging and frustrating in equal measure, she'd managed to expose the razor-sharp, sense of humor that he'd been capable of wielding with equal dexterity, at targets as diverse as small-town Texas, his fraternity brothers back at U.T., and the world at large. Unearthing his sense of humor had kept her at it long after she should have had enough sense to give up the challenge.

It had also made forgetting Alex and going on with her life one of the hardest things she'd ever done, but she had . . . until he'd turned up five years later in Nicaragua.

Megan had recognized at once that everything was the same: her feelings for Alex, as well as his lack of any feelings at all. Even the discovery that Eden Franklin was really Megan Davies had only provoked a slight twitch in his jaw, hinting at his displeasure—when any normal man would have yelled. Though his icy glare had been a warning of Lord-and-the-Agency-only-knew-what, she'd found herself goading him, trying to elicit some genuine reaction, just as she'd done in Florida. Instead of rising to the bait, he'd clammed up even tighter before dumping her at the base camp, heading off to his next assignment, and leaving her to pick up the pieces again.

And she had. Before Paris, she'd actually dared to believe she was through with him. When she'd run into Alex there at, of all things, an embassy dinner in honor of Mickey Mouse, inspired by the then-in-the-works plans for EuroDisney, it had shattered that tenet completely. Though Alex was, if anything, even more controlled, more emotionless, than before, her attraction to him had been stronger than ever. That recognition had been so unnerving, she'd fled, not merely the party, but the country, before she'd had a chance to do something a lot more stupid than what she'd done between Nicaragua and Paris.

This time, the barriers that had stood in her way then were gone. She had to get back to Himeros and away from Alex as soon as she could, before she made a complete fool of herself and begged him for something she knew he couldn't give . . . even if he wanted to.

*NO, MEGAN, ANY WARM body is not preferable.*

Mere seconds after he'd said those words and stormed out of the room, an alternative meaning, one that had been completely unintentional, became glaringly apparent to Alex. Judging by the expression on Megan's face, she'd come up with it immediately. It would have occurred to him, too—and before he'd said it—if his brain had been in control of his mouth at the time.

Groaning, he slumped against the cool wall of the cave and wondered how the devil she could do this to him. It wasn't like him to say or do *anything* without thinking it through, studying all his options, and weighing the consequences. She'd always had that effect on him; it didn't make sense, but then nothing else about this situation ever had, either.

During the fifteen years that had passed since his junior year of college, he'd had plenty of time to theorize about what had happened in Fort Lauderdale. Under the circumstances, it was hardly surprising that he'd come up with some pretty outlandish hypotheses. It wasn't easy for a man to understand why an inexperienced-but-beautiful-and-intelligent young woman would spend a week engaged in a sensual marathon with a stranger and then vanish without a trace. He could have sworn she'd felt it was something more, just as he had by the end of that time.

Just as he'd never been able to figure out why she'd done it, he'd never been able to find her—not until he'd been sent to Nicaragua to rescue an archaeologist named Megan Davies. By that time, he'd been with the Agency for three years—long enough that the obvious should have occurred to him before then. He hadn't been able to find Eden Franklin because she didn't really exist. The woman he'd always thought was Eden Franklin was Megan Davies.

While finding out she'd lied about her name resolved the question of his inability to find her, it had made the question of *why* she'd done it that much more perplexing. Frustrating, too, because he'd been called away before he'd had a chance to pursue the issue. By the time he'd tied up the loose ends on that assignment, satisfying his curiosity hadn't seemed nearly as important as his newfound certainty that a week in Florida had been all she'd ever wanted from him. He'd told himself to forget about her and move on. Let somebody else go and get her the next time she was up to her butt in trouble.

God knew, however, that it had bothered the living hell out of him every time some other agent had been sent to rescue her. On each of those occasions, the only thing more inevitable than a plumbing connection somewhere in the vicinity had been his own incessant need to find out everything he could about both the assignment and Megan. His sole consolation had been that he'd been able to spare himself the ultimate indignity of asking a lot of questions that would have made him *look* like an enquiring mind who *wanted* to know.

While the Agency had begun to admit women in recent years, amid much tooth-gnashing by old-timers
like Frank and his father, it was still, for the most part,
male territory, with an understandable tendency toward "locker-room talk." And, if there was one thing
in this world that might have been created for the ex-
press purpose of stirring up such talk, it was a six-foot-
tall blonde who couldn't manage to stay out of trouble
for more than a couple of months at a time.

Like most locker-room discussion, it was undoubtedly less fact than fantasy—men talking big for the sake
of having everyone within listening range think *they*
were big men. Any reasonable human being could see
it, and so could Alex—most of the time. There had been
times, however, when not even the fact that he had yet
to hear anyone mention Megan's mole had been enough
to assure him that there wasn't a man who had rescued
her who didn't know precisely where her mole was. Ir-
rationally, the only thing that had kept him from acting on those suspicions and throttling someone hadn't
been either his better judgment or his sorely tested self-
restraint, but the awful possibility that he might discover his suspicions had some basis in reality.

Though the mental image of Megan nuzzling up to
another man had been painful enough before he'd seen
her in Paris, after that, it had been almost unbearable.
When he'd tried to talk Frank out of sending him to
Zoman, it had been because he didn't want to know
how much worse it could get if he saw her again. There
had never been any question in his mind that it would.

He'd been right, but, Lord knew, he hadn't gotten a
bit of satisfaction out of being right. Seeing Megan
again, touching her, feeling her long, lissome body be-

neath his, had resurrected all the old feelings with new, even greater intensity. He didn't doubt that the next one of his fellow agents who mentioned her legs, even in the most innocuous of terms, was going to wind up in Intensive Care.

Damn woman. At the same time that he wanted to lock Megan away someplace safe so no one would ever have to go and get her again, Alex wanted to volunteer for permanent rescue duty.

Maybe he could just compromise and kill her.

# 6

BY THE TIME ALEX emerged from the back of the cave, Megan was genuinely *glad* to see him. Not that she'd wanted to see quite so much of him, of course, but, under the circumstances, that couldn't be helped. He retrieved his jeans promptly, tugging them on as if he were as eager as she to have his vital regions under wraps. Since his nudity wasn't a surprise this time around, she managed to avoid a replay of the night before by busying herself with making breakfast.

When she was sure he was decent, she turned to confront him with the reason she'd anxiously awaited his return. "I just went out to the mouth of the cave and . . . Alex, it looks like we might have some trouble getting out of here."

"The entrance collapsed?"

The choked sound of his voice and the aghast expression on his face were both so phenomenal, Megan almost wanted to let him go on believing it. Silently reproving herself for that impulse, she clarified, "The Zomanis moved again last night. Closer, from the sounds of it."

"Got any idea who's retreating?"

Megan glared at him, wondering if she should have bothered to enlighten him. "Does it really matter? Either way, I'd be safer without you."

"Only if your idea of safety is spending the rest of your life wearing harem pants and being guarded by eunuchs."

"That *wouldn't* happen, Alex. I've got . . ."

"Letters of safe transit from both sides," he completed, his voice patronizing.

"But they're as good as useless with *you* along. How could I possibly explain what you're doing here?"

"If you had to explain me to anyone, you could always say I'm a colleague," he suggested with a shrug.

"Right." The word reeked with mockery. "As if anyone would actually believe that *you* were an archaeologist."

"Is that so hard to believe?"

"Try *impossible*, Alex. There isn't a soldier in this world—regular army *or* revolutionary—"

"Freedom fighter," he corrected automatically.

With a see-I-told-you smile, she finished, "Who wouldn't recognize precisely what you are, the minute we ran into them."

"You know, Megan...the idea is *not* to run into them in the first place."

"You think I don't know that?"

"If you knew it, then why the hell didn't you stay on Himeros where you belong?"

"What am I supposed to do, Alex? Postpone my career until the world becomes a safer place for tourists?"

"No, but you could try showing a little common sense and avoiding unstable places, for a change. Do you think I wanted to come to Zoman and get you out of here?"

"So, why'd you do it?"

"I was ordered to come and get you, just like I was ordered to go and get you out of Nicaragua ten years ago."

Megan flinched at the mention of Nicaragua, but Alex went on, ignoring both her reaction and the opportunity to dig at her again about that trip. Apparently, he had another agenda.

"Just like Slater had to get you out of Iraq, just like Morelli had to get you out of Armenia, just like—"

"There was an earthquake in Armenia!"

"And if there hadn't been an earthquake, the country would probably have been invaded by locusts."

"Do you think I do this on purpose?"

"I don't know. Do you?"

Megan didn't answer him in words, but the forceful manner in which she flung the metal plate at his belt buckle told Alex just as plainly that the subject was closed. If she'd aimed a few inches lower, he wouldn't have been able to speak about anything for a considerable length of time. Eyeing his plate of eggs, he poked at them with his fork. "What's in here?"

Without pausing a beat as she filled her own plate, Megan answered, "Eggs."

He bit back the impulse to smile. While there couldn't be more than a handful of men in the entire world who were willing to provoke him, she went out of her way to do exactly that, time after time. She always had. "And these lumpy things?"

"*Kasseri* and *zampon.*"

"Which are?"

She looked up from her food, which she had yet to touch, her blue eyes challenging him. "You've seen those little brown and green lizards running around in here?"

Alex considered the contents of his plate and then Megan, as if deliberating the suggestion. The pretense was purely for her benefit; he didn't believe for an instant that she'd chased down the little beasties and killed them with her bare hands. He put a forkful of eggs in his mouth, chewed, and swallowed. "Tastes a lot like ham and cheese."

She glared at him as if she'd take great pleasure in killing *him* with her bare hands.

He simply smiled. "You're not a bad cook, considering what you've got to work with here."

Megan's expression shifted, turning skeptical. "When'd I ever cook for you?"

"This morning. Last night."

"I meant real food, Alex. Not instant."

"The *pollo con arroz* in Nicaragua." He started to chuckle, recalling the incident that had assured him he was eating ham and not lizard. He'd swiped a live chicken from the Sandanistas and the bird had put up such a squawk, he'd had to wring its neck before he'd gotten ten feet with it. He'd then told Megan that since he'd caught and killed it, plucking, cleaning and cooking it were up to her. After several pithy suggestions about what he could do with the bird, she'd gone ahead and made the meal. "I didn't think you were gonna be able to eat it after you finished cleaning it."

She sniffed and scowled at him balefully, her perspective of the incident being less amusing than his. "You didn't have any problems, as I remember."

"Strong stomach," he countered.

*Or no feelings at all*, she thought, though she didn't voice the sentiment aloud.

"I grew up on a ranch, Megan. If we let ourselves get too attached to the animals, it would've been awful tough to eat them afterward. Cows, chickens, rabbits . . ."

"Bunnies?" she squeaked, recalling the white rabbit she'd gotten for Easter one year during her childhood.

"Yes, bunnies. It was all the same to us. They were just food." Alex shrugged as if her revulsion was incomprehensible.

"Didn't you have any pets?"

"I had a dog."

Megan noted the past tense and was reluctant to ask what had become of the animal. The notion must have been reflected on her face, since Alex sighed and added, "Shiloh died in his sleep when he was seventeen years old. Peacefully, and of natural causes."

She wasn't sure whether or not to believe him.

"For God's sake, Megan, you don't think I'd eat my own dog, do you?"

When she didn't answer, just stared at him suspiciously, he shook his head, pushed himself to his feet, and reached one hand down to her plate. "You through with this?"

She looked up at him questioningly.

"You cooked, I clean up."

Now, *that* was unexpected. Alex doing kitchen duty. It was an intriguing concept, contrasting markedly with all the stalwart machismo. She handed over the plate immediately, before he could change his mind. "You know how to do dishes?"

"I know how to do *lots* of things."

She knew that. She remembered more than a few of them in intimate detail.

"This means that *you* get to pack up so we can leave as soon as I'm done." Alex turned away from her, took the dishes to the jug of water, and began to clean them.

"Pfft." Megan was well aware that it was the more onerous of the two tasks, due to the illogical but scientifically proven principle that clothing and sleeping bags expand once they're used, making it impossible to get them back into the same space in which they'd fit before leaving home. She glared at his back for a moment, and then smiled at the recollection that the things one picked up along the way were often the real problem. The smile lingered as she collected their gear and packed it away for the long hike out of Umal.

THE LACK OF SLEEP MUST have been harder on him than he'd thought, Alex reflected several hours later. It seemed as if his backpack had doubled in weight since the day before. It didn't make a damn bit of sense; going down was *supposed* to be easier than up, not the other way around. Checking his watch for the third time in as many minutes, he assured himself it wouldn't—couldn't—be much farther to the town where he'd stashed the Land Rover. As far as he was concerned, they couldn't get there one second too soon.

Not just because of his aching back or Megan's presence, either; the Zomanis still posed a very real threat, in spite of all the reassuring signs that the action was headed back down to the desert. Although the occasional spates of gunfire had come from that direction, there could be reconnaissance troops that weren't shooting…right now. Like everything else, that could change at any time.

At least Megan was capable of keeping up the pace, when most women would have crumpled up in an exhausted heap. Clearly, she was used to both the exertion and the altitude, and fit in a way that went beyond mere appearance. The last time they'd stopped for a break, she hadn't even been breathing hard. She'd broken into a sweat, though, and its dampness had glued the finely woven cotton of her loose white shirt to her body, rendering both it and the bra beneath virtually transparent. She'd seemed oblivious to her fundamentally naked state. He certainly hadn't been.

His mouth had gone dry at the sight of her breasts straining against the soft fabric, confirming what he'd suspected the night before. They *were* fuller than they'd been fifteen years ago. Not by a huge amount, but enough to challenge the claim he'd made then that more than a mouthful was a waste. They'd fill his palms now, while her nipples were still as pink and tight as he remembered. He'd wanted to unbutton her shirt, bare them to his eyes and hands and mouth, see them, touch them, taste them—so badly, it had made him ache. For that matter, he still did.

As if someone out there could sense Alex's distraction and thought it was the perfect opportunity to impress him with danger, a rocket suddenly squealed across the path below them and then exploded on impact. While the missile had landed some distance away, it was close enough to raise the question of whether it was aimed at them or was merely a stray. He didn't take the time to find out before grabbing Megan's arm and scrambling for the shelter of a nearby pile of rocks.

This time, Megan went with him voluntarily. Alex might not be her favorite person in the world, but he was the only currently available expert on the subject of heavily-armed hostile people. In the nerve-splintering silence that followed the boom, she whispered, "Where are they?"

He shook his head and frowned. "With rocket launchers, it's tough to say, exactly, after only one shell."

"You're telling me we *want* to hear more of them?"

"One only tells you where it's going, not where it's been."

As if in reply, another whistling sound commenced, followed by another blast. Though she wanted to cover her head and pretend it was simply a bad dream, Megan watched as Alex's eyes tracked the missile and then expertly retraced its route back to its origin. She didn't like to admit it, even to herself, but having him here at this moment was a comfort.

By all reports, there was no one more proficient at getting out of tight spots than Alex. It also seemed as if he intended to protect her, in spite of everything. As the second rocket had raced past, she'd felt his arm tighten on her waist and realized he'd covered her body with his, shielding it from the dirt and rocks that skittered over them. It was a noble gesture, one that made her feel guilty about having put *all* her specimens of concrete in his pack.

"See that?" he pointed out a moment later. "It looks as if they're a couple miles to the west. My guess is, they're taking potshots at that bluff to see if they can flush anybody out."

"Mmm-hmm," Megan answered.

"If that's what they're doing, this shouldn't take long," he continued. "Either they'll get something or they won't, and if they're way off base, they'll want to move before the other side can pin down their location." Shifting his weight off her, he turned to present her with his back. "Do me a favor and get the pistol out of my pack, will you?"

As Megan dug out the pistol, she was careful not to let any of the specimens rub together. Even with most of Alex's attention directed at the rockets, he'd never miss the distinctive sound, and that was one revelation she didn't think wise to make at that moment. She wanted him to defend her against possible attack by the Zomanis, not hand her over to them. Not to mention that armed and angry, he might decide to do it himself.

When she gave him the weapon, he checked it with competent familiarity and wedged it into the top of his jeans beneath his fly. Although she'd seen that handy placement of a gun numerous times on television and in movies, she'd never before considered its possible consequences. It was a tight fit, she observed with a surprising amount of concern. One false move . . .

"Megan?"

"Huh?" Megan's face went hot and her gaze shot up to his, mortified. The last thing she needed, after last night and this morning, was for Alex to catch her staring at his crotch.

Thankfully he didn't comment on it, though she was certain he'd noticed. "That last shot—" she vaguely recalled hearing another squeal and blast while she'd been gawking, and guessed he meant that one "—sounded as if they're moving out already, so they must be coming up dry. If we just stay put for a while . . ."

In her opinion, staying put sounded every bit as risky as walking into the line of fire. Even as he'd told her he thought the Zomanis were retreating, Alex had rolled on top of her again. His arm was back around her waist, the gun—she *thought* it was the gun, anyway—was poking into her backside, and his mouth was next to her ear, sending gusts of warm air across it with every word he spoke. If she had to endure this torturous proximity for very long, she was going to lose her mind and do something rash—like jump him.

While it didn't come to that, they remained huddled behind the rocks far longer than Megan would have liked. At last, when the silence lasted long enough to satisfy Alex, he told her, "We're gonna have to keep our eyes open, just in case, but I think it's reasonably safe to start out now."

As he rolled away from her and cautiously began to get to his feet, she turned to look at him and gasped. "Alex! When'd you get hit?"

"Hit?" he repeated blankly. "I wasn't . . ."

"The blood on your head." She flinched, not because she had a weak stomach, but because it was Alex's blood. Lots of it.

His hand moved to his head and came away blood stained. Looking down at his fingertips in a somewhat bemused manner, he said, "I wasn't hit, unless you count scatter."

She counted scatter, if it drew blood. Stepping toward him, she insisted, "Let me look at it, Alex."

He shook his head. "It's okay, Megan. I'm all right."

"No extra credits for bravery." She hesitated, wondering why the words seemed so familiar, then blushed as she remembered. Judging by his amused smile, Alex remembered, too. As determined not to succumb to embarrassment as she was to examine his injury, she sternly repeated, "Let me look at it."

For once remarkably acquiescent, he sighed and sat down on the ground. "Go on, then. Look."

With a silent reminder that scalp cuts bled profusely, all out of proportion with either the size or severity of the injury, Megan began to poke through his hair, looking for the wound.

She found it, and he expressed his suffering in a string of profanities before reining in his harshness to ask, "Well, what's the verdict?"

"This could really use a few stitches to close it—"

"You're not thinking of . . ."

"But I don't have the stuff to do it," she finished, and he sighed with profound relief.

"Do you think you can make the last couple of miles into town if I just patch it up?"

He nodded. He'd made it farther than that before, and with worse injuries, too.

"Okay, then." After shedding her pack and retrieving the first-aid kit, she returned to tend to Alex's wound. Kneeling beside him, she opened a small brown bottle and warned him, "Now this is gonna sting a bit."

"So what else is new?"

She glared at him and he shut up and steeled himself for it. In spite of that, he sucked in his breath and went rigid when she poured the liquid over his scalp. When he could speak again, he gasped, "What's in there?"

She shook her head and shrugged. "I don't know. No one knows but Gus—he makes it himself—and he's keeping that secret to himself."

"Who's Gus?"

"He's the cook at our dig."

"Who'd he train with, the Nazis? The Vietcong? My God, that stuff is wicked."

"I know, but it works," Megan replied, frowning at the cut on his head in a way that made Alex wonder just how bad it was, and then she started to work on it.

Though it hurt, he blocked out the pain by concentrating on the sensation of his cheek resting on the sleek length of Megan's thigh as she separated the matted strands of hair, pulled the cut closed, and bandaged it. By the time she wound gauze around his head, he was half aroused, due to several minutes' consideration of the mole on the inside of her thigh. His awareness of exactly how close the tiny brown circle had been to his mouth had been a chief factor in pushing him over the edge.

Coming to her feet, Megan asked, "How do you feel now?"

Alex repressed the first answer that came to mind. "I'll be fine. Help me up."

As they started down the mountain again, Megan couldn't help thinking it was just as well Alex was inclined to lead. It made it that much easier to keep an eye on him, in case he passed out before somebody who actually knew something about medicine took a look at his head.

A short time later, she reflected idly that keeping an eye on Alex wasn't what she'd consider hardship duty. Though the pack covered most of his back, his arms and shoulders were visible, and she could see the soft fabric of his shirt, sweat-soaked and dusty, adhering to his skin. Like wet-drapery sculpture, the sinewy muscles beneath were revealed in exacting definition; she'd never fantasized about peeling the material off a classical Greek statue, however.

His jeans, too, were molded to him so closely, it confirmed that his rear was just as tight and firm and well shaped as she remembered. She also remembered how it had felt under her hands, and that was maddening, given her current inability to reexperience it. Despite his injury, the excessive weight in his pack, and his apparent intention to arrive at his destination as rapidly as possible, he walked with the long, lazy stride indigenous to cowboys—or Texans?—she'd always found so appealing.

Caught up in that reverie, which was not interrupted by any more close encounters with either Zomani faction, she lost track of how far they'd gone until they were nearly into the village, whose name loosely translated as "Village at the base of the mountains guarding the ancient Roman city of Umal." Though she was a Christian woman, an infidel, she knew its devoutly Muslim residents would still be offended by her arrival in shorts, with her head bare. When she realized how close they were, she called out to Alex, and then hurried to catch up with him. "I should change into my skirt and scarf now, before we get any closer. Get them out of my pack, would you?"

She turned, giving him access to the flap. When he hesitated, she twisted her head around and immediately grasped the reason for his hesitation. Most of her colleagues—and all of the diggers—were men, so she was too familiar with this phenomenon not to recognize it for what it was. "I promise, Alex. There's nothing in there that might embarrass you. No feminine-hygiene products."

A flush crawled up his neck and across his cheeks and she almost giggled. She'd *never* seen Alex blush before; if anyone had asked, she would have sworn it was a physical impossibility.

At last, Alex began to unfasten the flap. When he found the clothes and handed them to her, she headed toward an outcropping of rocks for cover while she changed. As he watched her go, Alex trembled as if he'd contracted a fever. It had nothing to do with his injury, but was an uncontrollable reaction to the subtle scent emanating from the clothing in her pack. Not perfume, but the distinctive essence of her body. The smell was so evocative and tantalizing, it took most of his fortitude not to follow; the remainder of his willpower was expended in quelling his response before she returned with her skirt on and her shorts in one hand. Before she could give them to him to replace in her pack, he turned and suggested, "Just stuff them in here."

"Okay." Shrugging, she tucked them in his pack and refastened it. "Give me a second, and I'll be ready."

As Megan looped the long scarf around her head in a manner that reflected years of residency in countries where such things were taken as a matter of course, Alex watched the operation with pure fascination. There was something strangely, primally female about it that didn't, strictly speaking, make sense to him as a man raised in the Western tradition, but it affected him on some deep, subliminal level. Despite the fact that he'd already seen every glorious inch of Megan's body, he suddenly found the idea of veiled secrets very alluring.

EVEN THOUGH MEGAN WAS dressed decently by their standards, Alex was sure her appearance in the village still gave the locals plenty to talk about. Middle Eastern women didn't argue with men, at least not in public. Megan, however, did. Twice.

For the two of them, both arguments were relatively minor, since no one went for the cheap shot. Alex supposed she took it easy on him because of his injury. Actually, the injury was the cause of both altercations. The first, concerning whether or not he should seek medical attention in the village, was settled when he pointed out that the community was so filthy, he'd rather stick with her rudimentary first aid for the time being than expose himself to Lord-only-knew what kinds of exotic bacteria. The second, inevitably, was over who was going to drive to the airport at Tel Mapur; Alex had never liked riding with someone else behind the wheel, but he finally conceded that a head injury was sufficient reason for him to relinquish the keys.

Ten minutes later, he wished he hadn't given in so easily. No injury was severe enough to make him drive worse than—or even as badly as—Megan. By all indications, it had been a long time since she'd driven on a real road. She drove too fast, bumping over knolls and into holes with a reckless abandon that made his head ache even more. As a piece of chrome flapped around, tore off, and whizzed past his head, he assured himself Uncle Sam really wouldn't hold him liable for minor damages. Or even major, he added, as she found a particularly deep crater and tested the suspension system. He didn't say a word about it, but then, with Bruce Springsteen singing "Born to Run" at top volume, it would have been pointless to try.

They arrived at the airport an hour later, driving the same route that had taken Alex more than an hour and a half the day before. By then, he was convinced the harrowing ride had taken several years off his life, receded his hairline a couple of inches beyond "high forehead," and resulted in the shutdown of his nervous system. At least she couldn't insist on flying the Agency jet, too.

DURING THE FLIGHT TO Athens, he called Washington to report in and made an announcement that was so utterly unexpected, the only person more surprised than himself was Frank.

"You're taking a *vacation?*" Alex didn't need to see Frank's face to know his eyebrows were at their highest elevation. "So what, may I ask, brought this on?"

"Got a problem with it? I haven't had one in three years."

"I know. That's why I'm wondering what's wrong."

"Nothing, Frank. I just think it's time."

"Oh. Staying in Athens?"

"Actually, I thought I'd go out to the islands. Do some diving, get a tan, relax . . ."

"Any island in particular?"

Frank was fishing; Alex knew it, and he had no intention of indulging him. "Look, Frank, the plane's landing. I've gotta go. I'll call you in a few weeks."

"Alex!"

Alex broke the connection, knowing Frank wouldn't stoop to returning the call.

A half hour later, in the Athens airport, they tracked down the helicopter pilot Megan had said usually ferried them and their supplies out to the island. Alex wondered just how often that was. Clearly, the pilot knew her well. In a flurry of Greek, not one word of which Alex understood, he greeted Megan with a hug and kiss that took her right off her feet—no small accomplishment for a man several inches shorter than she. In his mid-thirties, attractive in a swarthy Mediterranean way that suggested ancient Spartan soldiers and athletes, Alex hated him on first sight.

When Megan finally remembered Alex's presence and introduced them, she had to serve as translator between him and Niko, whose last name was long and began, Alex thought, with a *P.* Each time she made the change to Greek, she stayed in that language longer; she also laughed more than when she spoke in English. Niko knew Megan *very* well, Alex amended with a streak of irritation.

As he and Niko stowed their gear in the chopper, the man flashed him a wide smile that displayed perfect too-white teeth. The masculine triumph in it transcended their lack of a common language, reminding Alex of his filthy clothes, his desperate need for a shave, and the bandage wrapped around his head. In spite of the sudden desire to correct those things immediately, he forced himself to get into the helicopter, put on the headset, and strap himself into the back seat with the luggage. To his added annoyance, Megan didn't have to do any of those things for herself because Niko solicitously helped her into the copilot's seat beside his own.

Once they were in the air, Alex scowled out the window, oblivious to the clear blue water beneath them.

Just what was this Greek Romeo's relationship to Megan? And who the hell did he think he was to hit on her when there was another man with her, albeit in the back seat and completely forgotten? And were those teeth real?

In the front seat beside Niko, Megan noted the conspicuous silence behind her, though she repressed the urge to turn around and investigate the reason for it, telling herself it would be a waste of time and energy. Considering that it wouldn't be long before Alex could leave her on Himeros and head out on what she was sure he'd consider some *real* assignment, he did *not* appear to be a happy camper.

Maybe he had a headache. His injury, which still hadn't been looked at by someone with more than basic first-aid skills, would certainly entitle him to one. Maybe he was tired. It was a plausible-enough excuse; he'd hauled forty pounds of concrete down the side of a mountain, after all. And maybe he'd already opened his pack. God, she hoped not.

They weren't in the air long before Megan spied Himeros, a sparkling white jewel against the cerulean waters of the Aegean. As the helicopter got closer, she was finally able to distinguish with increasing clarity details and finer gradations of color, each as vibrant and distinct as the individual gleaming rays within the lustrous depths of a diamond: the yellow variegations of the cliffs; patches of green denoting the sites of the sparse vegetation; the white gold of the sandy beaches, punctuated with sprinkles of brilliant scarlet and royal blue fishing boats and sails; and the clump of terra cotta that marked the island's only small village.

Across from the village was the excavation site, distinguished by olive-drab tents, the orange X of the helicopter pad, and the great brown slash of the dig itself. Though the sight was one Megan had seen repeatedly, she was torn, as always, between the need to learn the secrets of the past and regret for the impact of that invasion. While they tried to keep damage to a minimum, it was impossible to eliminate it completely.

Once Niko had landed the chopper, Megan and Alex retrieved their packs and the supply crates, dumped them in a disorderly heap on the ground, and ducked beneath the whirling blades as they ran toward the group of men who had gathered for its arrival. Safely away, they turned to watch as the helicopter rose into the air.

Alex emitted a silent sigh of relief at the departure of Niko and the chopper. He was glad to see the last of the man, and that his farewell to Megan hadn't been nearly as ardent as his greeting. Perhaps he'd overreacted, just a bit. Maybe they were merely friends. Probably, he assured himself.

A moment later, his irritation surged up again, fed by a fresh new source, as the men from the dig greeted Megan with the same fervent embraces—some that also included kisses, he noted sullenly—the pilot had earlier. As he hovered nearby, everyone chattered excitedly, simultaneously, in at least four different languages, none of them English or Spanish, which he knew because it was virtually a second language in Texas.

Alex frowned. Who were all these men? More important, who—and what—were they to Megan? He wondered if he'd been precipitous in coming to Himeros before finding out whether or not she was involved with anyone else already. Was she the only woman here, for God's sake?

Just as he was beginning to think he should have gone back to the mainland with Niko—or never gotten off the jet in Athens in the first place—one of the men on the edge of the group called Megan's name. As she looked up, her jaw dropped in apparent astonishment, and then she smiled so delightedly, she positively beamed. She rushed over to him, squealing with an excitement that contrasted dramatically with Alex's memory of the manner in which she'd greeted his own arrival in Umal. "Matt! My God, what are you doing here?"

The man, who was several inches taller than Alex, bringing him close to six-and-a-half feet, slipped his arms around Megan's waist, pulled her against him, and gave her a kiss that was entirely too intimate to qualify as merely friendly, even by the most liberal of definitions. "Meg, honey. How've you been? They said you went to Umal. Find lots of good stuff?"

She kissed him back. On the mouth. The others had only been kisses on cheeks.

"What are you doing here?" Megan asked again, still smiling up at the man. Although they'd each backed up a step, their arms were still touching in a loose embrace.

"Jean-Claude found some Close- and Fringed-Style pottery and wanted me to take a look because he wasn't sure whether they were Late Minoan or Helladic."

She nodded as if the answer made perfect sense to her; it made as little to Alex as had her earlier conversations in Greek and God alone knew what other languages.

Looping one arm casually around Megan's shoulder, the man turned to Alex and extended his free hand in welcome. "I don't think we've met. I'm Matt Sabin."

Alex accepted the proffered hand unwillingly, left with no other alternative, because refusing would have been churlish. In a voice that carefully concealed his aversion to both the cordial gesture and the man's casual affection for Megan, he returned the acknowledgement. "We haven't. Alex Sullivan."

Because his eyes were fixed on the hand resting on Megan's upper arm, Alex noticed the sudden stiffness that began there and quickly spread throughout the rest of her body. The other man, apparently oblivious to her tension, gave her shoulder a familiar squeeze and said with a congenial grin, "Meggie's a cutie, isn't she? I guess that's why I married her."

# 7

*MARRIED HER?* AS THE words echoed in his mind, Alex forgot how to breathe. When, at last, his deprived organs screamed for oxygen, he dragged air into his lungs and his eyes leaped up to Megan's face, seeking confirmation or denial of the claim. Her ashen complexion, her fallen jaw, and the stricken expression in her blue eyes all corroborated it.

An instant later, she made the effort to speak, but all she was able to force out was a croaked, "Alex..."

Not only did he not need verbal affirmation, he didn't want to hear her say the words. Not out loud. Though it took every ounce of the rigorous self-discipline his father—and then the Agency—had instilled in him over the years, Alex assumed an expression of stolid indifference. Before his tenuous hold on it could slip, he gave a brisk conciliatory nod to Matt, turned, and strode away from the pair.

As Megan watched Alex's departing back retreat across the compound, she started after him but stopped a step later, Matt's hand still on her shoulder.

"Damn, Meg, I'm sorry."

She whirled around to face him, angrily batting away his hand. "Impeccable timing, Matt."

"I always had it, didn't I?" he admitted wryly, his eyes shifting toward the other man, who was rapidly putting distance between them, and then back to Megan as he said, in a matter-of-fact tone, "That's him, isn't it?"

She sucked her bottom lip between her teeth and nodded reluctantly, though there was no reason not to tell him the truth.

Matt sighed eloquently and muttered an even more eloquent curse.

"My sentiments exactly," Megan agreed. Alex being Alex, he was probably on his way to find out what the local policy was on public stonings. If his opinion of her had been low before, it had undoubtedly just taken a nosedive so deep, it would have to be measured in fathoms.

"Want me to go fix it?"

Megan shook her head, though it was tempting to let him face Alex's anger in her place. It was highly unlikely he'd listen to *any* explanation right now, from anyone, whether or not it was the truth. "It might be better to let him cool down first and then talk to him."

"*Try* and talk to him," Matt amended helpfully.

"*Try* and talk to him," she concurred.

"Better give him *lots* of time," he advised. "Is a case of Double Stuf Oreos enough to earn your forgiveness?"

"You brought me a whole case?" When he nodded, she tipped her head to one side and smiled impishly. "It's a start."

ALEX DIDN'T STOP UNTIL he ran out of island. Fortunately, there wasn't much of it. Sinking down onto a rocky outcropping that overlooked the ocean, he wished he had a cigarette, though he'd given them up cold turkey seven years before. Or a stiff drink, though he rarely indulged in such self-destructive excesses.

He should have figured Megan would marry some-one—someone else—eventually. It wasn't as if he had any claim on her—at least, nothing official and bind-ing. Nothing more than the fact that he'd been first; and he wasn't sure anymore what that meant, if it meant anything at all.

It wasn't like him to be uncertain, but, every time he'd seen Megan, it had turned his life upside down, wreaking havoc with his composure and putting him in a state of turmoil that had lingered for a very long time after she was gone. On the flight to Athens, he'd suddenly decided enough was enough and, the next thing he knew, he'd told Frank he was taking a vaca-tion. He'd intended to come to the island and settle it once and for all—make things right with Megan or bring them to a definitive end so he could forget her. He didn't need to be going through this again in another five years.

Alex had known it wouldn't be easy, but the only thing that ever had been easy about Megan had been getting her into bed in the first place. Beyond that, she'd always been the most infuriating complication in his life, making him feel and do things he didn't under-stand. When he'd decided to come to Himeros, how-ever, he'd never counted on the complication of a husband, and that was one thing he didn't intend to mess with. He might not be a saint, but he did have his standards. Megan belonged to another man and that, as they say, was the end of that. All that was left for him to do now was go back to camp, pick up his things, and get off this blasted island and back to Washington. And when he said goodbye to Megan and her husband, good old Matt what's-his-name, he was going to be civilized about it if it killed him.

Which it might.

"DAMMIT, MEG, WHAT'S he got in here, anyway?" Matt demanded as he hoisted Alex's pack onto his back.

"Oh, Lord!" With everything else that had happened, getting the specimens out of Alex's pack before he found them had slipped her mind. She leaped toward Matt, tugging at the flap and nearly knocking them both over.

"Meg . . ." he accused knowingly, counterbalancing with ease now that he'd determined the problem. "He doesn't know they're in here, does he?"

"Do you really think he would have carried them if he did?"

"I always made you haul your own souvenirs."

"Would you shut up and help me get them out of here?" she hissed. Taking the pack, she dropped it to the ground with a thud, flipped up the flap, and began to drag out its contents.

"You certainly seem to know your way around in there," Matt remarked as she dropped clothing, assorted pans, and the pistol in an untidy heap on the ground.

"I ought to. I was the one who packed it."

"Yeah. Sure."

She glared at him, daring him to make some further comment. Although he didn't take her up on it, he looked at the pile, saw a pair of shorts that looked vaguely familiar, hunkered down next to Megan, and picked them up for a closer look.

"Give those back!" she snarled, reaching for the shorts she'd put in Alex's pack after changing into the skirt.

"Tsk, tsk, tsk," he scolded, shaking his head and holding them behind him, out of reach.

As she strained to retrieve them and failed, she growled through her teeth, "Dammit, Matt!"

"Uh-uh, Meggie." Matt dropped the shorts on the ground and sat on them Indian-style, thwarting her efforts. "Not until you tell me how they got in his pack."

Ignoring both the demand and the fact that the odds were clearly against her, Megan tugged at the snippet of fabric that stuck out, but the rest of the garment was too firmly anchored to follow. After several frustrating attempts to extricate them, he made a mocking noise at her efforts. Exasperated and annoyed, she retaliated in a manner that, while cruel, was also effective.

"Ouch!" Matt yelped and jumped as her nails, short yet surprisingly sharp, dug into his ribs at their most vulnerable spot. By the time he returned to earth, the shorts were in her hands. He rubbed at the sore place, gave her a wounded look, and emitted a whimper that implied she had done irreparable harm.

"Don't you give me that," she admonished him. "It doesn't wash anymore."

"Damn." He didn't sound either surprised or particularly pained by the contention as he reached beneath the last of the clothing to get to the bottom of the pack. "At least you had the decency to put the heaviest stuff at the bottom. Probably would have killed him if you hadn't."

"Would you hurry?"

Matt hauled out the first chunk of concrete and dropped it into a bin Megan had brought out of the supply tent.

"Be a little more careful with that, would you?"

"C'mon, Meg, it's not exactly as fragile as red-figure vases." He retrieved several more pieces and then hefted the pack several inches off the ground, testing the remaining weight. "Did you leave *anything* there?"

"Of course I did."

He stopped what he was doing, looked up at her, and shook his head with a wry expression on his face. "I think I remember why we aren't married anymore."

Megan and Matt both remembered precisely why they weren't married anymore, and it didn't have a thing to do with concrete specimens or who was going to have to lug them from the farthest limits of the civilized world. Their marriage had been doomed right from the start, primarily because it had been a big mistake for them to get married in the first place.

The decision had been an impulsive one, made when they were working together at a dig in the Cotswolds in England. They'd just discovered the remains of a Roman bath and were waiting for scientific verification. It was Christmas. It was raining and everyone was bored, depressed at being far from home during the holidays, and wishing the rain would change to snow. In a sequence of events neither could recall with any real accuracy, Megan and Matt's long-standing friendship suddenly escalated into romance, the rain abruptly turned to snow, and they got married in an equally spontaneous flurry of holiday spirit before either of them could really think about it.

It wasn't very long before they both recognized that it wasn't as terrific an idea as it had seemed at the time. No matter how hard they tried—and both really did make the effort—neither could raise the level of their feelings from affection to love. While affection had been a strong-enough foundation for a friendship, it wasn't enough for a marriage.

They probably would have acknowledged that fact and called it quits before long anyway, but, eight months after the wedding, Megan went to Paris and ran into Alex Sullivan. Her shaken reaction confirmed the doubts she'd already begun to have about the marriage; additionally, she recognized that the main reason she couldn't fall in love with Matt was that she couldn't forget Alex. Once she'd gotten back to Delphi, where they'd been situated at the time, she'd told Matt the whole story and, in a surprisingly civilized conversation, Matt had admitted that he'd always suspected there'd been someone in her past she'd never been able to forget; he'd recognized the symptoms because he'd had them himself. Megan had been no more surprised than he had been.

Wishing each other the best and agreeing to remain the friends they'd been before they'd made the mistake of getting married, they'd split up their few assets, gotten a divorce, and gone their separate ways. Since then, they'd settled into a camaraderie that no one, including their friends, colleagues, and families, could say they understood.

"Are you sure you don't want me to talk to him?" Matt again offered as he put the last of the concrete chunks into the crate and repacked Alex's clothing with a good bit less order than Megan had. "Find him, at least?"

"I'm sure," Megan answered. "It's a small island. How far can he go?"

At that moment, the subject of their discussion arrived on the scene, rounding the corner of the supply tent. Matt saw him first. "Speak of the devil . . ."

Megan looked up and tried to gauge the current level of Alex's displeasure. It was a fruitless endeavor, like trying to determine the mineral composition of concrete samples by sight rather than with the appropriate scientific instruments and methods; in both cases, visual analysis didn't provide sufficient data. Closer examination didn't help, as Alex proved when he approached her, stopping near where she crouched on the ground.

"If you have a few minutes, Megan, could we talk?"

Still watching Alex warily, she nodded and rose to her feet in a long graceful glide he couldn't help noticing. She might be married, but that didn't mean he couldn't look, as long as he didn't touch. He had enough touching on his conscience already.

"Let's go and get some coffee," she suggested. He nodded, figuring that gave him a few extra minutes to figure out exactly what he was going to say.

Those few minutes went by too fast. By the time he was seated at one of the picnic tables outside the cook tent, staring down into a cup of steamy coffee that was as dark and thick as molasses, he still didn't know how to begin—or, better yet, avoid—this conversation. Grasping at any available excuse to delay the start of it, he waited for Megan to pry open the top of a cardboard box sitting on the table, dig out a bag of cookies, and take a seat opposite him. At last, fresh out of legitimate reasons for stalling, he said, "About this morning, Megan, I..."

Megan inhaled sharply at the same instant she lost control over the cookie bag. Instead of pulling apart the seal, a troublesome task under the best of circumstances, she split open the entire cellophane wrapper, sending fat brown-and-white cookies rolling in all directions. With a cry, she scrambled to herd them back together.

Alex caught one stray as it rolled toward the edge of the table and another just as it plummeted over the brink. Although he thought that perhaps he should wait until they finished the cookie roundup before he continued the discussion he didn't want to have, he said, "Megan, I didn't know you were married or I—"

"*Were* being the operative word."

"—wouldn't have touched you," he continued, not hearing her because he was intently struggling to get through what he was saying. He was lousy at emotional analysis, and he knew it. His mother had always said he got it from his father.

"We're divorced."

"If we can just get a hold of Niko— What'd you say?"

"Divorced," she repeated firmly, nodding as she returned the last few intact stray cookies to the package with entirely too much attention to the task. "Four years ago."

"But...?" Sidetracked from his original objective, it could be any length of time before he managed to say something else.

"You're not alone. My mother and father don't quite get it, either." With the last of the remaining cookies more or less returned to their original order, she took one, twisted it apart, and scraped the filling off one half with her teeth. "It was an amicable divorce."

*To say the least*, Alex thought. To conceal his reaction, a mixture of pleased surprise and confusion, he raised his cup and took a tentative sip of the coffee. Despite the meager amount, he choked on it. While it looked like molasses, it tasted like he'd always imagined motor oil would. Motor oil that had been subjected to high engine temperatures for ten thousand miles, like the commercial said. Maybe twenty.

Megan was dunking one chocolate half of her cookie, now denuded of its filling, into her own coffee when Alex started to cough. While most people's reaction would have been to circle the table and start pounding on his back, Megan calmly popped the cookie into her mouth and waited for him to finish.

Alex sputtered and struggled for breath. As far as he could tell, the toxic sludge they passed off as coffee around here had seared his throat shut. All evidence to the contrary, he assured himself that if he'd survived armed terrorists and a whole spectrum of other job-related perils, he would also survive noxious coffee. At last, his paroxysm began to ease up, dwindling until all that remained were a few scattered coughs and a prickling moisture in his eyes.

"You get used to it eventually." As if to prove the point, Megan picked up her mug and took a drink.

Alex watched her in fascinated horror and wheezed out, "Gus made this?"

She swallowed the coffee and nodded.

"The same Gus who made the stuff you put on my head?"

She reached for another cookie and nodded again.

"Who told this man he was a cook?" he demanded in a raspy voice that made him cringe inwardly. He was absolutely certain his vocal cords were permanently damaged.

"We didn't tell him. He told us."

"He lied."

"He cooks better than he makes coffee."

Before he could assure her that no one could possibly cook anything as unpalatable as Gus's coffee, a stocky middle-aged man emerged from the supply tent, balancing, with no apparent effort, two cases of canned goods on one of his massive shoulders. He called out to Megan and then started to say something to her. It no longer surprised Alex that the remark was in Greek, though it did surprise him when Megan replied, "English, Gus. Alex doesn't speak Greek, and I think it's starting to get on his nerves."

It was an astute observation, as well as being one for which Alex was grateful. He didn't like not being able to understand what everyone around him was saying, and it was starting to feel as if he were listening to some inside joke that wouldn't make sense to him even if someone went to the effort of explaining it.

"She's a nice girl, our Megan." Gus pronounced her name with a long *e*. "Pretty, too, right?" Ignoring the blushing testimony to her embarrassment, he looked to Alex for confirmation. When he didn't get it immediately, he demanded in a booming voice, "Right?"

"Right," Alex agreed, smiling at Megan. She was more than pretty, actually; she was an extremely desirable woman, even more so now that he knew she wasn't married anymore.

"She give you head?"

Alex's second sip, which he'd braced himself for, went down the wrong pipe and he choked again. This time, it was the question that had done it. "Ex—excuse me?" he managed to ask. He fervently wished Gus hadn't bothered to make the transition to English for his benefit.

"Your head." Gus circled one hand around his own head in a perfectly innocent gesture that illustrated his intended meaning. "The bandage."

"Oh. Yes," Alex answered in relief, reminding himself that English was not a first language for Gus, so the man couldn't possibly understand the American colloquial connotations of his question. Desperate for assistance, he looked at Megan, but he recognized at a glance that help wasn't forthcoming from that quarter. Even if she'd wanted to help him out, he doubted she could speak. She was having so much trouble fighting back her laughter, there were tears in her eyes and her entire body was shaking. "I fell and Megan bandaged it."

"Looks like one of hers." Gus turned to Megan and asked, "You have to cut much?"

"Cut?"

"Not a lot."

Although their answers were simultaneous and Alex's was louder, Gus only replied to Megan's. "Good."

"Cut?"

"I make you *souvlaki* for dinner, all right? With lamb?"

Before she could answer, Alex reached across the table and grabbed her forearm. "Cut what?"

Her eyes turned to him, bigger and bluer than the Aegean. For a single instant, he forgot about his question, until she hesitantly answered, "Your hair."

He jerked his hand in, pulling her upper body toward him. "You cut my hair?"

"Not much. No more than I had to. Just a little bitty chunk . . ." She held up her hand, her thumb and first finger an inch apart in what he sensed was an optimistic underestimation. "About this much."

To Alex, the "little bitty chunk" might as well have been shaving him bald. His hair was something he was sensitive about; while it was thick and mostly its original color, his forehead was just a shade higher than it used to be. That his father's hairline had possessed precisely the same configuration for the last thirty years wasn't sufficient reassurance that the alarming deterioration wouldn't continue. "You cut my hair?"

"You didn't want me to give you stitches," she reminded him reasonably. "Which, by the way, you should still get."

"I can put them in," Gus offered helpfully.

Alex's gaze slid back to the cook and then down to his mug while he considered the inevitable conclusion of this discussion. He assured himself the man *had* to be a better medic than coffee maker. Before he agreed, though, he had to ask, "Is there a doctor on this island?"

Although Alex was hopeful, he fully expected the negative answer he got.

ASHORT TIME LATER, Alex walked toward the area of the compound where the tents of the living quarters were. His scalp pulled painfully where Gus had put in the stitches, and his entire head throbbed; his only consolations at the moment were that the worst was over and the bulky bandage was gone, replaced by a small pad that just covered the wound. At least that was what they'd told him; he couldn't see it for himself.

The last person he wanted to see was the first person he saw: Matt what's-his-name. Megan's husband.

"I see Gus's been at you," Matt greeted in a friendly voice as he fell into step beside him.

*Ex-husband,* Alex reminded himself with an admonition to be nice. Even if they weren't married anymore, Megan still seemed to like him. "It was a close call whether the stitches or the coffee was more painful."

"He cooks better than he does either."

"Thank God."

"I hate to be the one to break the bad news to you, but..."

Alex came to an abrupt halt. *Bad news?* This whole trip had been nothing but bad news, except for the announcement that Megan and Matt were divorced. He couldn't imagine how it could get any worse. Unless...

"There's a shortage of bunk space around here and you're gonna have to share a tent with me."

Alex breathed a sigh of relief. While rooming with Matt wasn't on his list of experiences-not-to-be-missed, he'd been afraid Matt was getting ready to declare that he intended to get his wife back.

"Sorry about it, Alex, but we're fresh out of options here," Matt went on. "You can't move in with the diggers. Even if they weren't all native Greeks who don't speak English, it would screw up the hierarchy around here. Management mixing with labor and all that.

Helmut's not a possibility, either. His girlfriend got in yesterday from Düsseldorf, we haven't seen either of them since then, and we don't expect to till sometime the middle of next week. *Hearing* them is another question altogether, because they've been going at it like minks and they're only in tents. But we won't talk about that because we're both gentlemen."

Matt laughed and Alex joined in.

"And Jean-Claude and Ian..." Matt's voice dropped in a conspiratorial manner. "Well . . . let's just say they want their privacy as much as Helmut and Renata do."

If Alex had met Matt under any other circumstances or, for that matter, if Matt had been anyone else, Alex would have liked him immensely and suggested they adjourn the discussion to the nearest bar. As it was, however, he was too suspicious of his friendliness—and any feelings the man might still harbor for Megan—to trust him completely. He wished he could ask, but the very presumptuousness of the idea stopped him cold. Even if he thought Matt would probably tell him the truth, he wasn't sure he wanted to know. How, after all, could any man *not* want Megan?

"And Meggie's the only woman on the dig, so she's got the little single tent all to herself," Matt casually offered, though Alex hadn't asked. "C'mon, grab your stuff and I'll show you where our tent is."

Alex braced himself, reached for his pack, and moved to heft it off the ground. It didn't seem as heavy as before and he was so surprised by that fact, he almost lost his balance. With one hand still clamped around the shoulder strap, he stared down at it and wondered why. At last dismissing it as unimportant, he shrugged his shoulders and followed Matt.

ALEX DIDN'T SEE MEGAN again until dinner, which was,
as promised, lamb. It was not, however, like any lamb
Alex had ever eaten before. When his mother cooked
lamb, it had always been a traditional roast leg of lamb
with mint jelly; this was in cubes on skewers, like shish
kebab. Unlike shish kebab, it was also fiery hot, sort
of like Tex-Mex, but in a subtly different way. He
wished someone had cautioned him about it as he
reached for the bottle of beer beside his plate.

"Try some of the cucumber sauce," Megan offered,
clearly aware of his discomfort. He thought she looked
amused by it. So what else was new? "This batch of
peppers is a lot hotter than usual, and it cools it off. So
does the bread."

"It's okay," he lied, sounding as bad as he had when
he'd drunk Gus's coffee. His throat was never going to
recover from the combined effects. "I just wasn't expecting it."

"Get used to it," Matt, seated next to Megan, across
the table from Alex, advised knowledgeably. "They put
peppers on everything here. Even scrambled eggs."

"Sorta like Greek Tabasco," Alex replied with a nod
of comprehension. Back in Texas, everything, including scrambled eggs, was doused in the stuff, which was
set on every table at every meal as a matter of routine.

"And think of this as a Greek tortilla," Megan said
helpfully, handing him a piece of bread she'd torn off a
thick wheel that looked like a pizza without sauce.

Alex took a bite of the bread and noted that it served
the same function as a tortilla, cutting the heat of the
other food, as did the cold white sauce used like the sour
cream on burritos. He found himself wondering what
the Greek equivalent of refried beans was. He took an-

other sip of beer, assuring himself that some things, at least, were universal.

"So, how long are you staying, Alex?" Matt asked.

"I haven't really decided yet," Alex answered cautiously, wondering why Matt wanted to know. Was he hoping it wouldn't be for long? And, if so, why? He hadn't acted as if he wanted Megan back, but Alex was deeply skeptical of presuming the obvious, particularly where Megan was concerned. "Maybe a few days. A week or so. It depends."

*Depends on what?* Megan asked herself with a puzzled frown. At first, she'd thought Alex was only carrying out orders to bring her back to the island; it had surprised her when he'd stayed. She'd also been confused, irked, worried, and, in spite of her better judgment, just the least bit hopeful it might mean he wanted to be with her. She'd seen no indication that that was the case, however, even after she'd told him she and Matt were divorced. He'd spent the entire afternoon secluded in the tent he was sharing with Matt, apparently trying to avoid her.

No one else at the table paid the slightest bit of attention to either Matt's question or Alex's answer, and the language barrier wasn't the only reason for their disinterest. Jean-Claude and Ian were all wrapped up in each other, as were Helmut and Renata, who had presumably required refueling and come out of seclusion to fulfill that need. By all indications, it wouldn't be long before both couples went looking for privacy. Which left her and the two good ol' boys, who sounded as if they might go out taverna-hopping without her at anytime. It was, at best, a demoralizing prospect.

"Do you scuba dive?" Matt asked as he reached across Megan for another hunk of the bread and then dunked it in the juice from the peppers.

"A little," Alex replied, watching the process with clear fascination. "I got my certification three years ago."

Megan began to fidget uneasily. All he'd done since they'd sat down at the table was talk to Matt, pretty much treating her as if she were a piece of furniture. She was grateful the two of them hadn't wound up discussing choice of weapons and meeting at dawn, but this unexpected pals-for-life chumminess was too much like what she'd dreaded back in college. It almost sounded as if Matt had designated himself Alex's tour guide. Or, God forbid, his confederate. Matt wouldn't tell Alex everything he knew— Would he?

"You need a special license for tanks and diving in Greek waters, because they've had so much trouble with people smuggling things out for the black market. We've got a permit, though, and the tanks, so if you want to go, there's a great shipwreck on the other side of the island...."

*Male bonding*, she observed with disgust as Matt continued to tell Alex about the wreck. Though she'd gone down to see it soon after her own arrival, she didn't contribute to the discussion.

"Did Gus make baklava, or should we break out the Oreos?"

It took Megan a moment to realize that Matt's question was directed at her, rather than at Alex. It took her much less time than that to react in a hair-trigger manner that she recognized was irrational, even while she couldn't stop it. She told herself it was due to the combination of Alex's return, too little sleep, and the unnerving prospect of having Matt and Alex not only on the same island, but in the same tent—and seeming to like it. Rising to her feet, she glared down at them indignantly.

"They're my cookies. *Mine*," she repeated, emphasizing the word. "You keep your mitts off them. Both of you."

Alex and Matt stared up at her wordlessly, confused by her sudden outburst. When she stepped over the bench, turned, and stomped away from them with the same stiff acrimony apparent in her movements, they both watched her go and then looked back at each other.

"What'd we do?" Alex asked, puzzled. All through dinner, he'd sensed she was upset about something, but he hadn't been able to determine the cause. He still wasn't sure what it was, but he knew damn well it wasn't cookies.

"Got me," Matt replied with a shrug. "Maybe you'd better go find out."

"Me?"

"She's not my responsibility anymore."

"What makes you think she's mine?" Alex asked warily.

Matt shrugged again. "Instinct. Cosmic vibrations. The fact that you're still here instead of on your way back to the States."

Alex stared at Matt incredulously. No one had ever been able to read him so easily, and he couldn't imagine why Matt, of all people, would be the one who could.

"What do you want, Alex, written permission? If you don't get moving, you're gonna have to chase her halfway to Athens."

The statement triggered Alex's memory of the other times Megan had run off. While it didn't seem likely that she'd leave the island and disappear this time, right in the middle of an important dig, there was always the possibility she might be able find some means to do precisely that. Her track record certainly gave every indication that she could.

Alex got to his feet and went off in the direction she'd gone. As he rounded the corner of the supply tent, he heard Matt call after him, "Good luck!" He appreciated the generous sentiment, because he had a feeling he was going to need it.

# 8

SHORTLY AFTERWARD, Alex reached the conclusion that finding Megan on Himeros was going to be a lot harder than finding her in Umal had been. No plumbing connection here—or at least, not one worth following. While he was hardly an authority on the subject, he knew feminine pique generally required more quiet and seclusion than either the dig or the village could provide. The whole rest of the island, however, had nothing else *but* quiet and seclusion—acres of it, every inch of which Megan knew like the back of her hand.

In his frustration, the first five minutes of Alex's search seemed as long as the five years that had passed between each of their encounters, and he thought about just heading back to camp to wait for her eventual return. *But that's if she ever returns,* he amended disgruntledly, rejecting the idea. If that damn woman took a notion and got going, she could be halfway to Hong Kong by sunrise.

After fifteen minutes yielded the same lack of results, he seriously considered tracking down Matt and admitting he'd appreciate some help from someone who knew this pile of sand and rock—and Megan, perhaps—better than he did. As if his pride didn't like that idea much, he began listing good, logical reasons to tough it out alone a while longer. It wasn't dark yet. Himeros was only a tiny island, with no handy means of flight. Fifteen years was long enough to wait and he didn't want to try for twenty. For the moment, he refused to think about the question of what it was he'd been waiting for.

As if in reward for his perseverance, Alex was spared from having to contend with that question, when the faint sound of music drifted from the other side of a knoll. *The Eagles*, he noted with a smile of recognition. *"One of These Nights."* Some things never *did* change, thank God.

He saw her as soon as he crested the hillock—a dark shadow against the bright orange backdrop of the setting sun as she sat on the beach, her knees drawn up in front of her. The soft fabric of her skirt lapped around her in the breeze, while the last lingering rays of the sun gilded her hair with shimmering golden light. She looked so lovely it made his heart ache, and he paused to fix the image in his mind before starting down toward her.

The music, the surf, and the sand all muffled the stealthy sound of Alex's footsteps, but Megan still sensed his approach. Sensed *him*. It wasn't the vibrations of his tread that she felt, but some as-yet-unexplained sixth sense—like human radar—that told her he was near. Desire, anticipation and dread all welled up inside her, in spite of her most valiant efforts to suppress them. Because she knew looking at Alex would thwart them completely, she didn't turn her head, or even her eyes, away from the sea as she caustically remarked, "All right, Alex, I'm out of Zoman and back on Himeros, right where I belong and all in one piece. What the devil are you doing still here?"

As a greeting, it left a great deal to be desired; he might almost think she didn't want him there, if he didn't know better than to believe it was as simple as that. As a question, it was one he couldn't answer, any more than when Matt had posed the same question, in much friendlier terms.

Evading the issue, Alex dropped down onto the sand a few feet away, settled in as if he'd been invited to do just that, and asked, in a deliberately conversational manner, "D'you plan to make a lifelong career out of this?"

Megan quickly turned to stare at his profile, which was as expressionless as the head on an ancient coin. Frustrated by her inability to interpret anything he said or did, annoyed at the sharp stab of desire that shot through her, and flustered by the question that had turned the burden of defense back on her, she snapped, "A career? Out of what?"

"Running away. Waiting for me to follow. And then running again." Alex turned his head, looking directly into her eyes and holding them for no more than a heartbeat before he glanced away toward the shore and, beyond that, toward the setting sun. Megan wished *she* could escape that easily. "What is this, Megan? Hide-and-seek, with a little twist for the grownups?"

"I'm not running away," she said. Despite her certainty that Alex knew it for what it was, she clung to the lie like a lifeline. "And I'm not waiting for you."

"Liar." The word sounded more like a statement of fact than an accusation, but Megan flinched anyway, and felt her face heat with embarrassment. She hoped Alex hadn't seen either of those reactions, engrossed as he was in the process of gathering handfuls of sand and

letting it trickle out between his fingers. She waited
through several slow handfuls before he finally spoke
again. "Why'd you take off this time, Megan?"

She didn't know what to say, exactly. That the camaraderie between Alex and Matt was too close to the
kind of thing she'd feared back in college fifteen years
earlier? That she kept expecting the two of them to start
comparing notes? That she wasn't quite prepared to be
the subject of that exchange?

"Dammit, Alex . . ." she growled around the lump in
her throat. It wouldn't go away, no matter how much
she willed it to. . . . Sort of like Alex, himself.

"C'mon, tell me the truth for once in your life. I can't
read your mind, you know."

"That's funny. I always thought you could."

"If I could, I would've known your name wasn't Eden
right from the start," he argued reasonably; she would
have seen it herself if she'd been thinking more clearly.
"And it wouldn't have taken me five years and a trip to
Nicaragua to find you."

"You can't mean to tell me you tried."

The skepticism in Megan's voice washed over Alex
like icy rain, chilling him to the bone. Neither the balmy
breeze that drifted in off the Aegean nor the heat that
still radiated from the sun-baked sand could offset the
sensation. Inundated by it, he nodded wordlessly.

"Why?" she demanded, her natural tenacity fueled
by her disbelief.

"Why?" He didn't know what she wanted to hear, or
even what he wanted to tell her. Hell, he'd never been
able to figure out what to tell himself, and that should
have been a lot easier. "I felt . . . responsible for you."

"I never asked you to be."

"You didn't have to. It goes with the territory, especially when the woman's a virgin."

"You're telling me that the first woman *you* went to bed with has been keeping tabs on you all this time?"

Alex sputtered for an instant. "It's not the same thing."

"Sounds sexist to me."

"Maybe, but—" He broke off suddenly, considering her initial objection, which had nearly been lost in her digression into the subject of male chauvinism and double standards. Meaningless hostility again, just like before, and he'd always thought she was using it as a smoke screen. Now, he was sure she was. "You didn't *want* me to feel responsible?"

"I didn't want you to *have to* feel responsible," she said gently but firmly.

He understood the distinction, but wasn't sure he understood the point. If all she'd wanted was an extended one-night stand—fun and games with no strings attached—that was one thing; but why had she believed she needed to tell all those lies in order to get it? The things she'd said that morning came back to him in disjointed fragments, puzzling him even more now than they had then. *Revenge? Apologies? Any warm body?*

The music changed to the slow romantic melody of "Best of My Love" as Megan went on, her voice falling to a level that was nearly inaudible over the crash of waves against the shore. "Or obligated. Or—"

"Dammit, Megan, I *tried* to find you," Alex interrupted. "I looked for you everywhere after spring break, and it practically drove me out of my mind when I couldn't find you."

"It did?" Megan gaped at Alex incredulously. His claim that he'd looked for her because he'd felt responsible for her was in character and, therefore, believable. But the words "out of my mind" hinted at some far more compelling motive, and *that* was neither in character nor entirely believable. Unless . . .

"Of course, it did," he answered hoarsely, still sifting sand as diligently as if his current assignment was to comb the entire beach by daybreak. Though it went against all rational thought, she wanted to believe the project was a ploy to avoid meeting her gaze. "I wanted to see you and wondered where you'd gone. . . . At first, I couldn't understand it, and then I was hurt. . . ."

*Hurt? Alex? Could it be there really *was* something besides responsibility involved?* "You were?"

"Of course, I was. What man wouldn't be?"

And there it was, Megan thought, as the guilt and astonishment and hope she'd been fostering instantly withered. She should have known Alex's masculine pride had to be involved. As if it wasn't enough that he'd been nagged by his overdeveloped sense of responsibility, he'd also been incapable of letting go of the one that got away. Undoubtedly, it had been bred into him, along with his height and his drawl. Good ol' Texas machismo, the stuff that had made them hang on to the Alamo long after it was clear the battle was lost, didn't know the meaning of the words *Give it up.*

Calling upon every scrap of composure she possessed, Megan gathered her legs under her, began to rise, and said, in the most carefully-controlled voice she could muster, "I'm sorry I've been such a bother to you. It won't happen again. Goodbye, Alex."

Before she had straightened her knees, Alex caught her wrist and pulled her back down next to him again. "Goodbye?" he repeated. "What the hell does that mean?"

She jerked her head around, glaring at him as she struggled to free her wrist. Though his grip wasn't as bruisingly tight as the day before, it was every bit as tenacious. "It means that I'm leaving. Or you're leaving. One of us is, anyway."

"I'm not going anywhere," he retorted angrily. She tugged again, but he refused to relinquish her wrist. "And neither are you, until we give it another shot and see if you can come up with the whole truth this time. C'mon now, Megan, what *really* happened in Fort Lauderdale?"

"Look, I'm sorry I involved you in my little identity crisis, okay?" she snapped.

"Identity crisis?" Alex echoed blankly. If he didn't know she'd spent most of the last fifteen years working in places that didn't have cable TV, he'd swear she'd been watching too much Oprah. Frustrated by her continued evasiveness, Alex tightened his hold, forgetting both the bruises he'd given her the day before and his vow not to do it again. "Did you hear me complaining? Did you hold me prisoner? Did you rape me?"

"No! Gimme my arm!" Megan hissed, prying at his fingers, which still didn't give.

"Then you don't have a damn thing to feel sorry for. Not then and not now. You don't owe me any apologies, Megan, but you *do* owe me an explanation—and, this time, I want the truth."

Looking every bit as frustrated and furious as Alex felt, Megan blurted out, "Dammit, Alex, I was the last virgin left!"

While it appeared as if she thought the announcement said it all, it mystified Alex a great deal more than it enlightened him. He opened his mouth and closed it again, several times, unable to summon words in his befuddlement. Fortunately, he didn't have to find them for Megan to go on.

"Twenty-two women on my freshman floor, and I was the only one left. Back in high school, it was ... normal. There were the bad girls who did it, and the good girls who didn't. Even most of the girls who were going steady with somebody didn't go to bed with them. When we got to college, though, all that changed. It wasn't just good girls and bad girls anymore."

Alex knew what she meant. He'd dated his own high-school girlfriend, a very good girl, for three years, and they'd done everything *but* consummate the relationship, not because he'd been doing the honorable thing, but because she'd adamantly refused to cross that last line. Once she'd gotten to college, she, too, had renounced that rigid tenet ... though, as it turned out, it hadn't been with him.

"When we started school in September, most of us were still ..." She paused, swallowing heavily, as if the word were stuck in her throat. "Virgins. It wasn't more than a couple of weeks before the prettiest girls, the popular ones who never had any trouble finding dates, were all paired off, and everybody *knew* they were sleeping with the guys they were dating, whether they'd been good girls before or not."

So far, Megan wasn't telling him anything he didn't already know. Even at a school as big as U.T., it had been pretty much the same during those first few weeks after the arrival of every new freshman class. While he, for the most part, had merely watched the action from the sidelines, he recalled how the upperclassmen had scoped out the freshman women, picked the best prospects, and rushed in to stake their claims before the stars could fade from their eyes, enabling them to see things more clearly.

Alex also knew what had happened after the initial frenzy had subsided, but, with a brave candor that befitted a woman who would head into a war zone alone, Megan went on to remind him: the frat parties and dances that were basically meat markets; too much drinking, and by people who hadn't done a lot of it up to that point; the guys whose standards of beauty and integrity both became appreciably more liberal after two in the morning; and the girls who wanted to believe what they told them.

"And, every Monday morning, there were fewer and fewer of us left, like an endangered species that wasn't sure why it ought to be saved. By the beginning of spring term, even the women who weren't . . . pretty or popular . . ."

As Megan's voice wavered on the last three words, Alex's fists clenched against his outer thighs. After fifteen years of being torn up with frustration at *not* knowing the truth, he was stunned to discover he could be equally torn up by hearing it. He was far better equipped to handle confessions of the I-threw-the-bomb-that-blew-up-in-the-Belfast-train-station variety than those of a more personal nature.

"I was ready, Alex. So ready."

Now, *there* was one thing she hadn't needed to tell him; he remembered, all too well, how she'd gone off like fireworks the first time he'd touched her. Her response had been so immediate, so volatile, it was no wonder he'd never guessed she was a virgin until that fact was already past history.

"But I heard how the guys sometimes acted afterward. We all did. If the girl wasn't actually seeing the guy she did it with—if it turned out to be nothing but a one-night stand—she couldn't know whether he'd brag to all his buddies about how he'd made the big score or he'd act as if he didn't remember. And, either way, at a small school, everybody knew what had happened."

Alex nodded in grim understanding. Locker-room talk was only a limited edition of the grapevine. At a small school, he was sure it had been as pervasive, comprehensive and efficient as any communications network the Agency had ever devised.

"And then, after we heard that Jack Barnes told Trish he'd only gone to bed with her so he could say he'd been the one to pop the cherries of both the Maynard sisters, a friend of mine said it might be better if the first time was with someone she knew she'd never see again, because then nothing like that could ever happen to her. She wouldn't have to expect anything from him, she wouldn't have to wait for him to call, she . . ."

Alex's outrage at the first part, and who Jack Barnes and the Maynard sisters were was immaterial to it, was eclipsed by his reaction to the rest of it—the part he knew related directly to Megan. He didn't need to hear another word to know the rest of it. Megan's reluctance to be hurt by gossip or expectations that were never fulfilled had been so strong, she'd intentionally lied to him. He understood the sentiment, but wished she'd given him the chance to prove how wrong she'd been—about him, at least. While he couldn't say he'd been a saint, either during college or afterward, he'd never been one of those guys who kept score of their conquests or said they'd call and never did. And he definitely wouldn't have done it with her.

"When I saw you in Florida, I was attracted to you, and you seemed willing enough to do it...."

*Willing enough?* If he'd been any more willing, they'd have been arrested for doing it right there on the beach, in front of God and the Fort Lauderdale police and thousands of other college students on spring break. Even now, while his attention should have been focused entirely on the explanation he'd waited so long to hear, he couldn't help noticing the nervous way she kept chewing her bottom lip. He couldn't help staring at the swollen little tooth marks left behind. And he couldn't help wanting to soothe the inflammation with his tongue.

"I was so tall and skinny, I was afraid that no man would ever want—" Her hand flew up to press against her lips, halting the words and the lip-chewing at the same time.

*Megan had actually thought she was too tall and skinny for any man to want her?* Now, *there* was one of the great misguided notions of the century. Those magnificent long legs had been an integral part of any number of elaborate fantasies he'd constructed in the last fifteen years, and the talk among the other agents who had rescued her had made it abundantly and in-

furiatingly clear that he wasn't alone in his perception
of her desirability.

Alex didn't know why, how, or from whom she'd
acquired the notion that she was unattractive—had the
guys she'd gone to college with been stupid, or just
blind?—but it was clear that it had had a lot to do with
what had happened so long ago in Fort Lauderdale.
Everything, in fact. Judging by the things Megan had
said and done since his arrival in Umal the day before,
he got the distinct impression it wasn't entirely behind
her even now.

And he'd done his share of contributing to it, Alex
thought, recalling the things *he'd* said and done in the
past twenty-four hours. More than his share, even
though he hadn't known he was attacking her point of
greatest vulnerability. Whether or not it was inten-
tional, nothing hurt as much as a shot to a long-healed,
and ostensibly forgotten, wound. Afterward, she'd
turned around and given him first aid when he'd needed
it, too, though she'd had every reason to be mad
enough to abandon him there. Lord, what an appall-
ing mess.

So why was he wondering if—and more importantly, *how*—it could be fixed?

"Megan..."

She lifted her head warily as Alex finally spoke.
Nothing in her entire life—not the defense of her dis-
sertation, not the end of her brief marriage, not even
the original decision to make love with Alex—had ever
been this difficult. During the telling, she'd actually
been grateful for his silence. The only thing that had
kept her going, long after she'd really wanted to stop
baring her soul and giving Alex even more ammuni-

tion to use against her, had been momentum. If he'd interrupted, that momentum would have been lost, along with her tenuous grip on her composure, and she'd never have been able to go on.

Now, however, Megan wished he'd said or done something—anything—that would have given her some indication of what his reaction had been. *Before* the part about how tall and skinny she'd been would have been nice, because she'd *never* intended to admit that. As it was, she couldn't decide whether it would be smarter to launch an attack before he did, or burrow down into the sand like a shellfish tunneling to safety.

Before she could act on either of those inclinations, Alex continued, his voice strangely husky. "I've thought a lot of things about you in the last fifteen years, and I'll admit not all of them were nice. But the one thing that has never crossed my mind in connection with you—not once in all that time—is 'too tall and skinny to want.' Believe me, Megan, I wanted you in Florida. And God knows, I want you now."

In a single movement so fast and fluid that Megan never saw it coming, Alex moved over her, pinning her beneath him with her back against the sand and his lips covering hers. They demanded—and got—a response from her—one she couldn't restrain any more than she could control the automatic functions of her body. And, just as those involuntary processes were necessary for her continued survival, she *didn't want* to restrain these responses. She wanted Alex in the same way she wanted air or food.

A soft, hungry growl rose from deep in her throat as she raised her arms to his shoulders, slid her hands up his nape, and dug her fingers into his hair. She opened her mouth farther, taking everything he gave and greedily wanting more. She wanted to feel Alex's hands and mouth caress her breasts, her belly, the feverishly aching place between her thighs. She wanted to feel him deep inside her—so deep, his body would almost become a part of hers. She wanted to absorb him into her very soul.

At that thought, Megan's pulse quickened and she shivered with rising excitement. She could deny it until she was old and gray, but the truth was that the desire was still there, just as potent and all-consuming as it had been fifteen years before. No other man had ever been able to make her feel this way—as if she were going to go up in flames at any second. She longed to experience it again in all its glory.

She was caught between a whimper of deprivation and a gasp of discovery when Alex straightened his arms, lifting his mouth from hers and, at the same time, nudging his lower body against her. In a raspy whisper, he said, "I guess I don't have to tell you how much I want you."

He certainly didn't. Lying between her raised thighs, his body was hard with arousal against her softest, most sensitive regions. Reflexively, Megan shifted beneath him, slid her legs up his flanks, and tightened them, drawing him in even closer.

"Oh, God, Megan. Don't do that!" he groaned, though he made no effort to disengage himself.

She gulped and breathed, "I'm sorry, Alex."

He cursed under his breath and then muttered, "If you don't quit apologizing . . ."

She opened her mouth to say she was sorry for apologizing, but caught herself in time and stopped.

Although she hadn't said a word, Alex knew she'd been about to do it again. With a low chuckle and a shake of his head, he pressed himself against her, unnecessarily ensuring that she knew precisely what he meant, when he said, "I don't get like this for every woman, you know."

"I never said you did." Megan glared up at him, her eyes narrowed with suspicion and speculation and something else he couldn't name. He couldn't say any of them were auspicious, but that didn't discourage him. She hadn't started to shove him off her yet, or even lower her legs from where they gripped the outsides of his thighs, and that was a good sign.

"But you thought it." Before she could repeat her earlier accusation, Alex denied the absurd charge. "It doesn't take a mind reader to figure out that you believe all it takes for a guy to get it up is a warm body."

Her body, a lot hotter than warm, went stiff beneath his, and she let out an affronted squawk of protest.

"You said it yourself this morning," he reminded her evenly.

Megan angrily thumped her clenched fist against his chest. "And *you* said . . ."

He ignored the impact, merely curling his hand around hers and cradling it firmly against him. "I *meant* you were *wrong*. I want you, Megan. *You*."

She quit pulling at her hand and looked up at him, clearly still less than convinced of his sincerity.

"Don't you *know* how desirable you are?" He let her hand go and stroked her cheek with the backs of his fingers. The skin was so soft and delicate. He remembered, all too clearly, that the skin on the rest of her body was just as silky.

She whimpered softly and her hand opened to lie flat against his chest. As he felt the tension flow out of her body and she went warm and pliant beneath him again, he smiled, then bent his head so his mouth was close to her ear, and whispered, "You're so desirable. So beautiful."

Her heart jumped, skipped a beat, and then started to drum again in a rapid measure of her arousal, a progression Alex felt against his open mouth as he pressed it to the pulse point below her ear. When Megan tipped back her head, granting him greater access to her throat, he took full advantage of the tantalizing invitation. "The only woman I've ever wanted this much..."

While it was the oldest line in the book, Alex realized that, in this case, it was also the truth. He *did* want Megan more than he'd ever wanted any other woman. The desire wasn't simply a physical thing. Even more than he wanted Megan, he wanted her trust, complete and without reservations of any kind. Without that, making love to her again would only be compounding mistakes that went all the way back to that spring break in Florida. He told himself he had to stop... after just one more taste. Maybe two. He promised himself he was going to stop.

As his mouth covered hers again, he heard her low, wordless murmur, felt the quickening of her body, tasted and smelled the sharp tang of her passion—all sensations that did absolutely nothing to support his determination that he was *not* going to make love with Megan until things were more settled between them.

That it would happen sooner or later was beyond doubt, as far as he was concerned. While Megan might not trust him—*didn't*, if he was being honest about it— it was clear that she wanted him as much as he did her.

Lord knew, Megan wanted to believe him so badly it hurt. Hearing the uncontrollable sound of her own passion, she was torn between the impulse to believe Alex and the instinct to protect herself. So far, the impulse to believe him was winning, but then, it had the insistent demands of her body on its side. She trembled as one of his hands skimmed down her body to her thigh, then back up again toward the part of her that burned for his touch.

Her mind suddenly turned traitor, dredging up long-suppressed memories that were less evocative than explicit. The last thing she needed at this point when she was already more aroused and confused than she'd ever been in her life, was to remember *exactly* the way it had been to hold Alex on top of her and inside her at the same time.

The images were so vivid, so powerful, they elicited the most primal of reactions from Megan, as muscles deep within her clenched as if closing around him, releasing the hot flow of her arousal. She guessed she wouldn't have to tell Alex how much she wanted him, any more than he'd had to tell her. The irrefutable evidence of it was right there at his fingertips, if he moved them the merest fraction of an inch from where they were tracing the leg band of her panties. As she squirmed beneath him, it wasn't entirely clear whether her objective was to make sure he didn't touch her and establish that fact, or to make sure he did.

That heated internal debate was still going on when the source of the conflict was suddenly removed, rendering it irrelevant. As smoothly and swiftly as he'd covered her body with his, Alex pulled away from Megan and lay instead on the sand beside her.

*Now, what the hell was that for?*

Too stunned to move, Megan remained where she was, flat on her back with her knees raised and parted and her skirt hiked up around her hips. She shivered as the cool breeze streamed over and between her bare legs, grazing against her hot, moist flesh with all the shocking impact of an ice bath.

A pounding pulse and raggedly uneven respiration echoed in her ears for several very long moments before she realized that, while the heartbeat was her own, Alex was the one having trouble breathing. Turning her head, she gazed over at him and blinked several times, too baffled by what she saw to accept it at first. He was lying flat on his back, legs sprawled out and twitching slightly. Each time he took another breath, his chest heaved and then deflated again in several jerky movements. The arm that was flung across his eyes actually shook.

"Alex?" she asked softly, rolling onto her side and raising herself up on one elbow.

Slowly, he lowered his arm and turned his head toward her. The light from the recently-risen moon illuminated his face, and, although she couldn't say for sure exactly what the expression reflected, it *looked* like pain. In spite of her frustration, she couldn't help being encouraged by the possibility.

"Are you okay?"

With visibly strenuous effort, Alex dragged another breath into his lungs and let it back out again. When he finished, she got a better look at his face, and the expression she'd thought she'd seen a moment before was gone, obliterating her hopes. She should have known better than to expect anything else.

"Go back to camp," he ordered harshly.

Hoisting herself the rest of the way up to a sitting position, Megan reached out a hand toward him. "But . . ."

He yanked his shoulder away an instant before her fingertips touched it. "Please, Megan . . . Just go back. I'll be fine."

Incredibly hurt by his rejection, she snatched back her hand. How he could kiss and caress her senseless one minute and then not even want her to touch him the next was as much of an enigma as his ability to douse all evidence of an expression in the same amount of time. "But, Alex . . ."

"Don't make me explain now, Megan," Alex growled fiercely. "Just *go*. I'll see you in the morning."

So dazed she automatically obeyed, Megan slowly rose to her feet and started up toward the top of the ridge. Just as she got there, however, she stopped abruptly, turned around, and stalked back toward him. If he thought he could treat her like this and get away with it—again—he had another think coming.

"You want to know why I don't believe you enough to stop running? Alex, you expect me to tell you everything . . . show you everything . . . Everything, that is, that you can't tell just by looking at me. And then, just when I think I'm starting to make some progress— that you're starting to open up—you shut off the switch so fast, I can't help wondering if you ever felt anything at all."

She stomped her foot angrily.

"I'm sick of it, you hear? Sick of the macho silence, sick of the stoicism, sick of the whole damn thing. You say you want me? No, Alex, I don't think you do. For that matter, I don't even think you want a 'warm body.' What you really want is one of those inflatable dolls that won't expect too many things—like real, honest-to-God *feelings* from you. When you're done with her, you can let the air out and stick her back in your closet, knowing she'll still be waiting when you come back for her."

Turning away from him, Megan stormed off toward camp. Before she got to the edge of the sand, however, Alex rolled over and called out her name, and she paused just long enough to fling one final shot.

"I hear they're very lifelike these days. I'm sure the two of you'll be very happy together."

# 9

THE FOLLOWING MORNING, Megan was pale and exhausted when she arrived at the breakfast table. She'd been up most of the night, kept awake by the memory of what had happened—or, rather, what had *almost* happened—between herself and Alex. The only reason they hadn't made love was that he'd stopped it; Lord knew, *she'd* never have been able to. And that, of course, was the problem in a nutshell. While Alex might be—in fact, had been—the only man who'd ever made her feel as if her blood were on fire, he'd never be able to feel the fire himself.

*Damn the Agency, anyway.* If there'd ever been any emotions there, as she was idealistic enough to imagine from time to time, they'd trained Alex to survive and to switch them on and off, mostly off, as efficiently and instantaneously as if he were a machine.

*Damn Texas.* If the Code of the West—still thriving in that state long after most of the rest of the world had declared it an anachronism—hadn't been instilled in Alex since birth by his father and all those other macho Agency types, he might have learned to balance self-control with sensitivity, the way a few agents, like her father, had done.

*Damn Alex.* If he'd just said something—*anything*—when she'd screamed at him the night before . . .

Gotten angry. Yelled back. Run after her and grabbed her and tumbled her back down on the sand beneath him again . . .

He hadn't, though. She didn't know why she'd ever deluded herself into wishing he might.

Megan only hoped that when she saw him this morning, Alex looked every bit as lousy as she felt. If he looked as if he'd had a good night's sleep, it was going to be his last, because she was going to kill him, and this time she meant it.

"You look terrible, Meg. Didn't you get any sleep at all?" Matt asked, setting his plate on the table and then dropping down onto the bench opposite her.

Although she felt hot color rise in her cheeks, Megan glared at him, hoping he'd get the message. There were times she cursed the fact that she and Matt had parted on friendly terms, and this was one of them. She didn't want to discuss Alex with Matt, but knew he wouldn't let up that easily. As far as he was concerned, their relationship entitled him to certain liberties, as if, even now, he had some proprietary interest in her.

"Now, now, Meggie . . . Don't be like that." He scraped the peppers off his eggs with meticulous care, lifted a forkful, and inspected it for any he'd missed before popping it into his mouth. "So where were you hiding?"

"I wasn't hiding," she told him tartly.

"Then why didn't Alex ever find you?" He paused to study her face when she didn't answer and, apparently, read the truth in her expression. "He *did*? What the hell happened, Meg? You were back in camp *hours* before he was!"

"Matt, shut up. Just shut up." She leaned forward and pounded one fist on the table. "I don't want to hear..."

"You're not gonna let him get away again, are you?"

"Did I ask for your opinion? Advice? Nagging?"

He took another bite and then answered with an ingenuous smile, "No, but I never let that stop me before, did I?"

She called him a foul name. While the word could only be categorized as "gutter French," he knew what it meant and began to chuckle.

"You're probably right. Look, Meg, if you're not gonna give the man a chance, if all you're gonna do is chase him away, there wasn't a damn point in us getting a divorce. He seems like a decent guy. So why don't you cut him a break?"

She glared at him again and rose to leave. Before she went, however, she leaned forward and softly said the one thing guaranteed to end the discussion, a reprisal he'd left himself open for the moment he'd brought up their divorce and Alex in the same breath. "I could say the same thing about you and Nina, couldn't I? Why don't you give her a break?"

While the stinging remark had its intended effect, keeping Matt from saying anything else on the subject, Megan was forced to listen to Gus's unsolicited advice when they took the Land Rover into the village to the market. Like Matt's, it quickly escalated into nagging, and it didn't make it any more palatable for her to remind herself that Gus, at least, didn't know about her and Alex's past history.

As they walked past the fish stall, Gus remarked, for at least the dozenth time since they'd left camp, "Megan, he's a nice man. Very brave, too. He didn't make a sound when I put in stitches." This was high praise from Gus, who, while a reasonably competent medic, was a little on the rough side. Megan suspected that he'd considered it some sort of test of Alex's machismo—one he'd apparently passed with flying colors.

"How's the calamari today?" Megan asked the fishman, Spiro, in an effort to sidetrack Gus. "Is it fresh?"

"The freshest," Spiro confidently assured her with a big, nearly toothless grin. "This morning's catch."

Undeterred, Gus enlisted Spiro, who Megan was certain would agree with him wholeheartedly. Greece, like Texas, was holding out on the question of machismo, and macho men, as a rule, tended to stick together. "A man followed her back to Himeros, and now she chases him away."

"A man?" Spiro asked, obviously intrigued. He'd introduced Megan to every last one of his single male relatives under the age of seventy—a staggering number, even given the size of Greek families—and been disappointed when his matchmaking efforts had met with no success. "Not Maththaios?" Like the other Greeks on the island, he called Matt by the Greek version of his name. It had been a source of great frustration that Megan's name couldn't be Hellenized, too. "Who is he?"

"An American, like her. Tall."

"Taller than she is?"

It went without saying that Spiro's relatives had all been a full head shorter than Megan, as most Greek men were.

"Almost as tall as Maththaios."

"Why you chase him away, Megan?"

Megan closed her eyes and sighed, wishing both men would disappear before she opened them again. When she did, however, they were not only still there, but had been joined by Irina, the woman who sold baked goods in the next stall. Just what she needed—another interested party with no direct involvement or personal stake in the situation.

"Don't you want to get married again?" Irina demanded with a scowl. "Have babies?"

"What's the tall American's name?"

"Alexandros," Gus answered, his voice filled with pride not only at his own ability to provide that information, but at the information itself. The name was revered throughout Greece, due to the still-recent—by their relative standards—memory of Alexander the Great, the ruler who had unified the ancient Greek city-states and then gone on to conquer most of the Mediterranean and the Near East.

"Ooh!" both merchants crowed, plainly impressed by the name.

Recognizing the futility of arguing, Megan buried her face in her hands and shook her head. She'd be lucky if everyone on the island, including Father Theodouris, didn't know about Alex's presence and set on her, too, by the end of the day.

"A defender!" Spiro pronounced. "And a conqueror!"

"You should marry him!" Irina declared with a nod.

"I've been telling her that all day, but will she listen?" Gus contributed.

For a moment, Megan considered pointing out that the subject of marriage had never been mentioned and was one she could safely presume had never crossed

Alex's mind. It seemed like a waste of breath, however . . . or, far worse, the surest route to having them jump all over *him* next. Alex would probably blame *that* on her, too, and this time it really *would* be her fault. In an effort to divert their attention, she prompted, "The calamari?"

For a reasonably bright woman, she could be incredibly dumb sometimes. She would have been much better off keeping her mouth shut, and she should have known it. Calamari was a big mistake. Huge, actually.

"Ah! Calamari!" Spiro beamed happily before he confided, in a booming voice that was loud enough to share the information with most of the Mediterranean, "Is good for virility!"

WHILE MEGAN WAS BEING besieged by the locals, Alex stood atop the ridge overlooking the excavation and wondered where she could be. The other archaeologists, Helmut, Ian, Jean-Claude, and Matt, were all there, but he didn't see Megan. Surely she couldn't have found a way off the island this fast.

He wondered if she'd gotten any more sleep than he had, or if she was, perhaps, sleeping in late to make up for it. After he'd kept his promise to himself not to make love to her, and she'd flounced off the night before, he'd lain on the beach for hours, deliberating the things she'd said, trying to understand, and only becoming more and more perplexed about why she'd gotten so angry. He'd gone swimming, hoping the cool water would clear his head, but that hadn't helped, either. When, at last, he'd headed off to bed, he was no closer to knowing what had set her off than when it had happened.

Sometimes, he thought life would be a lot easier if that damned woman came with a code book.

Because thinking about it would accomplish nothing except to make his head start pounding again, Alex pushed the subject aside as he looked out over the dig. Somehow, he'd expected more than a hole in the ground that looked like one of the abandoned strip mines he'd played in as a boy. For that matter, it was smaller, shallower, and, on the whole, less impressive than any strip mine he'd ever seen.

Granted, the sum total of what Alex knew about archaeology could fit in the palm of his hand, but he'd expected there would be cranes and scaffolding. He'd envisioned a huge, bustling crew of workmen, ancient swords and vases and jewelry strewn about like long-forgotten toys, statues and bits of buildings, all waiting to be plucked out and hauled away to some museum. In short, he'd pictured a scene out of one of the Indiana Jones films.

He guessed there was no more truth in archaeology movies than in spy films, because all he could see was dirt. It looked as if they were building a swimming pool, albeit a funny-looking one, with levels of equal sizes but varying depths instead of a bottom that sloped steadily downward toward one end. Suspended above the hole was an orderly gridwork of strings, with bigger squares outlining the perimeters of the ledges and smaller ones dividing the individual ledges into smaller sectors.

Each of the archaeologists was working on a different level, digging with small tools that were little better than tablespoons and dumping the dirt into galvanized aluminum pails. To say the least, it didn't look like the most efficient way to dig a hole. At the rate they were going, they were all going to be too old to care by the time it got big enough to line with concrete, put in the water, and fire up the barbecue.

The one thing in the scene that *did* meet his expectations was that it was busy. In addition to the archaeologists, there were Greek laborers everywhere, fetching soil-filled buckets and exchanging them for empty ones, sifting the discarded dirt in a huge, mesh-bottomed box, and occasionally calling for one of the archaeologists to come and look at their latest find. Unnoticed in all the confusion, Alex watched Matt climb out of the hole to take his turn. As he poked at the rubble, frowned, and shook his head, Alex realized there was more to this archaeological stuff than walking around and picking up stray artifacts.

Once Alex circled the hole to the sifting site, Matt lifted his head, smiled in greeting, and said, "Just junk...again. It looks like the southwest corner's pretty well played out below the tenth century. That's B.C., not A.D.," he added, going on to explain how the dig was like an upside-down time line: The deeper they got, the older things were at that level. "Anyplace else, we probably wouldn't bother taking that section any deeper, but we have to go down to before the flood in 1500 to make sure, since a lot of sites were reduced or abandoned at that time."

While it was all very interesting, Alex had more important and, certainly, more immediate concerns on his mind than the flood of 1500 B.C. At the head of the list was how to bring up the question of Megan's whereabouts in a more subtle fashion than coming right out and asking if she was already on her way to Outer Mongolia.

As if reading Alex's mind once again, just as he had the night before, Matt grinned knowingly and offered, "Meggie's gone into the village with Gus. She doesn't trust him to go to the market by himself anymore. Not that anyone else does, either, since the eggplant disaster." Before Alex could ask, he added, "Gus's methods of economizing—translate that into cheap streak—are legendary around here. Last month, somebody made him a good deal on eggplant, and they all had to eat it for a week. Moussaka, eggplant Parmesan, stuffed eggplant, eggplant stew... and then he ran out of legitimate recipes and started using his imagination. I'm just grateful I got here late enough to miss the experience."

Without missing a beat, and certainly without warning, Matt changed the subject. "Out late last night, weren't you? I didn't hear you come in, and wasn't sure we'd see you at all this morning. Not that anyone would blame you."

Alex wished Matt had kept talking about food. If the man expected true confessions, he wasn't going to get them from him, and it didn't make a damned bit of difference that he'd been out late the night before, merely *thinking* about Megan.

Dismissing Alex's silence with a shrug, Matt continued, "Any man with half an ounce of common sense would know enough to duck and cover when Meg's on the warpath. I take it the two of you didn't settle whatever it was that got under her skin at dinner."

Though it was a comfort to learn he wasn't alone in his inability to understand either Megan or her mercurial temper, it was undermined by the implication that Matt knew they hadn't made love the night before. It was downright unsettling, and Alex would have felt the same even if the opposite had been true. In a gruff manner he hoped would deter Matt, Alex shook his head and replied, "No."

It didn't. Matt obviously didn't know a hint when he saw one, unless, of course, he was choosing to ignore it. "All you can do when she gets like this is just stay out of her way until she cools down."

But he *did* seem to know what he was talking about. Though it went against all his natural inclinations, Alex not only let Matt proceed with his advice, he actually listened to it, telling himself it would be foolish to turn down any source of help, no matter how unexpected and unlikely, without first hearing it out and judging it on its merits. It wasn't as if he were making great-guns progress on his own.

"Fortunately, it doesn't take long for her to storm it off and then get over it."

Thank God. Alex only hoped she got over it soon, because his vacation wasn't going to last forever. He didn't have a lot of leisure time to sit around waiting for her to forgive him for whatever it was he'd done.

"And was she storming when she came back! The whole camp couldn't help but hear her slamming things around and muttering."

Following his instincts, Alex glanced over toward the dig, where all activity had been abandoned in favor of watching his exchange with Matt as attentively as if it were their favorite soap opera. It was no consolation that Alex knew the discussion was too quiet for any of them, even the ones who did speak English, to hear from that distance.

"Some nonsense about damned fools and public castrations, if we heard her correctly," Matt added, showing no sign of noticing either Alex's reflexive male reaction or the audience. "I guess we did. She was pretty vocal about it."

Alex hoped Matt really did know what he was talking about. If he was mistaken in his contention that Megan raged for a while and then forgot all about it once she got it out of her system, he was in *very* big trouble.

"To be honest with you, Alex, I didn't even think you found her, she came back so much earlier than you did."

"I found her," Alex admitted, though he hadn't intended to tell Matt even that much. Somehow, it had just popped out of his mouth of its own volition. If he didn't pull himself together and watch what he was saying, the next thing he knew, he'd be spilling his guts to Megan's ex-husband.

"I know. Meggie told me this morning."

The way *she* was apparently doing, Alex thought, and the hackles rose on the back of his neck. So what other intimate details had Megan told him? For two people who weren't married anymore, they seemed to be mighty chummy.

"Right before she insulted me in three different languages, and stormed off in another snit. Look, I'd better get to work, or I'm never going to get back to my own dig."

"You're working somewhere else?"

"Bulgaria. We're mainly looking for export niello, although we'll take anything Mycenaean we can find at this point."

Alex nodded, although he didn't have the slightest idea what anything after Bulgaria had meant. "I'll see you later, then. I'm going for coffee."

"Masochist." Grinning at the accusation, Matt turned toward the excavation and then, a step later, turned back again. "Alex, I'm not the problem. You know that, don't you?"

"You're not?" Alex couldn't stop himself from asking.

"Nope. Megan is. And I think you are, too."

AN HOUR AFTER ALEX went to the cook tent for another cup of the vile brew Gus alleged was coffee, he was bored to the point of distraction. While the state had actually commenced a half-hour earlier, it had taken him that long to identify it. He wasn't used to doing nothing and was relatively certain he didn't know how. He hadn't been on a vacation in three years, and then, he'd spent it taking scuba lessons. The year before, he'd helped reroof his father's barn. And before that . . . Well, suffice it to say, he'd always *done* something on the few vacations he'd taken. He wondered what other people did to keep from going stir-crazy on theirs.

He'd already made up his cot, unpacked—where *had* he picked up all that sand and gravel?—and had breakfast. He'd then taken a hike to the excavation site looking for Megan, but she hadn't been there. Taking what comfort he could in the fact that she hadn't left the island altogether—yet—he'd come back to camp for was supposed to do now, after the novelty of relaxing had worn off, he didn't have a clue.

Although he hadn't checked with the local tourist bureau, if there was one, which he doubted, he was fairly sure there wasn't much in the way of things to do here. No golf course. No tennis courts. No nightlife of any kind. If this was peace and quiet, he'd had more than enough of it already, and he hadn't even been on the island twenty-four hours.

He hadn't expected Himeros to be Club Med, but he'd expected being with Megan would make it bearable. Lord knew they hadn't found any shortage of things to do in Fort Lauderdale, and they hadn't even seen the beach again after the first day. While he'd never dared to hope that would happen this time, he'd had an idea that spending time together would steer them in that general direction eventually. Instead, according to Matt, she was making plans to ensure he wouldn't get there, ever again, as long as he lived. Talk about strategies going awry. Maybe he ought to leave now, before she got any madder.

It wasn't part of his nature to give up, however, any more than it was part of his nature to relax and do nothing. Like his other vacations, this one had a purpose. He was going to make things right with Megan. He was going to convince her that she was not only beautiful and desirable, but the woman he wanted more than he'd ever wanted any other in his life. After fifteen years, he was absolutely certain of this. And then, when she believed him, he was going to make love to her until the memories of Florida paled in comparison.

It was a commendable ambition. All he had to do was find her first.

The night before, Matt had mentioned a small, team-property scooter. Once he located it, Alex noted that it was small, all right, as well as rusty, dented, and twenty years old. It was also the only means of transportation available while Gus and Megan had the Land Rover.

As Alex eyed it warily, it wasn't his ability to ride it that concerned him; years before, back in Texas, he'd had a big old Harley hog that made this thing look like a kiddie toy. It wasn't the lack of a helmet, either; he'd had his bike in the days when riding without one had been legal, and he'd been too young and arrogant and, looking back on it, stupid to worry about risking his skull.

What really filled him with doubts was whether or not the vehicle was capable of making it into the village and back again. If he was lucky enough to make peace with Megan, it might only have to make it one way, but he didn't want to count on it. And, by the looks of it, even that would be stretching the limits of its durability.

Mentally crossing his fingers, Alex straddled the scooter, turned the key, and kicked the starter; after grinding unhappily, it coughed, turned over, and immediately stalled. As he repeated the process, he muttered under his breath, telling himself that getting to the village would, if nothing else, keep him occupied, and therefore not bored, for a good part of the day. His second try was more successful, and as he gunned the throttle to keep the engine from stalling, he decided that it sounded better than it looked.

The scooter failed to live up to that initial promise. He'd never expected it to run like his Harley, but he'd told himself speed didn't matter. That, of course, had been before he'd been passed by a flock of sheep that had left him eating its dust and wondering if walking mightn't have been faster.

At the edge of the village he caught up with the sheep, who were held up by a traffic jam of goats that were as determined to get out of town as the sheep were to get in. The scene of livestock gridlock was a familiar one, taking him back to the days of his Harley. He skirted it with ease and went into the center of town.

There wasn't much to it, but then, he hadn't expected much. Only the sound of his motor and a boom box playing 2 Live Crew assured him he had not been transported back through time to some earlier century. It looked like a village where one would expect to find sheep and goats wandering loose. Smelled like it, too, though the distinctive aura of fish also hung in the air. The people were all dressed like peasants, wearing the same styles of clothing their ancestors had worn for hundreds of years: women in full skirts and blouses, with sandals on their feet, men in baggy trousers and shirts with scarves tied around their necks. As he rode through town, keeping an eye out for the Land Rover, they all turned to look, nudged each other, and pointed at him.

Just as Alex was starting to feel as if he'd forgotten his pants back at camp or done something equally deserving of all the attention, he saw the jeeplike vehicle Gus and Megan had driven into the village. After pulling in the scooter, he noted that the back seat held several baskets of fruit and vegetables, none of which, to his eternal gratitude, was eggplant. He was deliberating whether he ought to wait there for Gus and Megan to come back with another load or go looking for them when he heard a man call out, "Alexandros!"

Since his arrival on the island, Alex had managed to pick up enough Greek to recognize his own name when he heard it. Raising his head, he looked around for Gus, the most likely source of the congenial greeting, but didn't see him anywhere. Instead, there was a little old man he'd never seen before, who smiled and waved at him as if he were a long-lost cousin. Telling himself that he must have seen Gus—unless Megan had spent the morning recruiting a hit squad among the locals—if he knew who *he* was, Alex headed toward the man.

Though he was standing in front of a stall filled with baked goods, Alex was never in doubt that the man was actually a fish seller. The smell of fish made seeing them unnecessary. While his senses kept insisting that he was as close to the man as he wanted to be, he forced himself to ignore the odor. The way things were going, he couldn't afford to alienate anybody; he might need every friend he could get.

"You are Alexandros, no?" the man asked. "Megan's American sweetheart?"

Well, he was an American. As for the other... "Yes. You speak English?"

"A bit, yes." He nodded and smiled again, revealing a grand total of six teeth. "I am Spiro. Gus tells me about you. That you are brave and you bring Megan back from Zoman."

Behind Spiro, an old woman, shorter, fatter, and even more toothless, said something Alex guessed was a question. He couldn't understand it, because it was in Greek, as was Spiro's rapid-fire argumentative reply. The woman, clearly unsatisfied, continued to badger the man, until he turned to Alex with a weary sigh. "Women. You know how they are."

Alex certainly did, although that didn't mean he understood them. As he was about to tell the fish seller that, the man cut him off, asking, "Irina wants to know you marry Megan?"

Flabbergasted, Alex stared at the man as he rearranged the words in every possible order, trying to make sense out of them. He figured that Spiro's English was probably as faulty as Gus's, so what he'd said might not be at all what he'd meant. At last, he decided the same response he'd given Gus the day before was probably his best bet now. "Excuse me?"

"You come here to marry Megan?"

Reworded, the question established that it had not been the inadvertent end result of Spiro's limited command of the English language. What he'd said *was* what he'd meant. Alex only wished that coming up with an answer were that simple. "I came to see Megan," he replied cautiously.

Irina tugged at the fish seller's arm, obviously demanding a translation. When she got one, however, it was equally apparent that it didn't suit her; with a frown, she launched into a long, heated tirade that Alex was grateful he couldn't understand. It didn't let up until Spiro, with no more than one raised hand and a growl, abruptly ended it. Impressed beyond words by the crude but effective technique, Alex was still gawking at the man when he spoke again. "Big, strong man like you should marry Megan." He grunted and nodded adamantly.

"I..." Alex began. He wished Spiro had let Irina continue. At least her badgering didn't require an answer.

"Like Amazon, she is!" He extended one arm over his head in a reasonably accurate approximation of Megan's height.

"I..."

"Maththaios is good man, too, but not *anima* enough to handle wife like her." He shook his head and sighed.

"I..." Alex tried again, and then stopped to consider the concept. He couldn't imagine anyone "handling" Megan, because she wouldn't stand for it for one minute.

"You make good strong babies together!"

Alex stopped his efforts to speak and stared at Spiro, wondering if, in the absence of Megan's father, he was going to start negotiating a bridal price and, if so, how many goats and sheep he was going to demand for her. Just as he was about to ask, purely out of curiosity, a sharp, outraged howl sounded behind him.

"Spiro!"

Megan advanced on the little man, ranting with such displeasure that Alex didn't need to know a word of Greek to understand it. At first, it was amusing, primarily because it was directed at someone else and not him. But when she turned on Gus, her voice reflecting that she blamed him for whatever Spiro had done, Alex acknowledged that, while he wasn't the target of her wrath this time, he was definitely the reason for it. Or rather, the notion of marrying him was.

So, what was so utterly intolerable about that?

The question slammed into Alex with the speed and impact of a Pershing missile, and its aftershocks were just as cataclysmic. What *was* so awful about the idea? By most standards, he could be considered a pretty decent marital prospect: a steady job with a good income, not bad looking, still had all of his teeth and most of his hair... And he knew Megan responded to his touch—and he to hers—as if they'd been made for each other. So why was she acting as if someone had just suggested she volunteer to set up shop in a war zone? What *had* made her so mad at him?

"Megan..." he ventured.

Hearing the voice of the person he knew she least wanted to talk to, Megan whirled around to turn her venom on him. She was so furious, it took her several moments to realize she was still yelling in Greek, and she switched to English. "Why don't you just go back to Washington, to your nice, safe little world?"

*Safe?* He'd never heard his job described as "safe" before, and he opened his mouth to tell her that. Before he could say a word, she continued.

"Sure, they shoot at you, but emotionally it's as safe as life gets. You just do what they tell you and don't think about things like emotions or feelings or..."

"That's not fair, Megan," he quietly objected.

"It's not? The guys at the Agency certainly knew what they were doing when they picked you. They didn't want a human being. They wanted a robot."

# 10

A *ROBOT?* ALEX RECALLED angrily as he rode back to camp on the scooter. After their latest skirmish, asking Megan for a lift hadn't seemed like such a good idea. Matt's report that she'd been advocating public castrations was still fresh in his mind, and he wasn't about to take a chance on her being serious as long as his name was at the head of the list of prospective candidates.

What the hell had he done to make her that mad?

The common thread between the accusation she'd flung at him in the market and her rampage of the night before had been clear to Alex, but that didn't mean he understood it. Where had Megan gotten the idea that he didn't have any feelings? He had them, just like anybody else. He was, after all, only human, as she'd proven time after time, shooting his self-control straight to hell with a consistency that would shame the range scores of most of the Agency's finest marksmen. He couldn't explain, let alone contain, the way he behaved when he was around her.

It had always been that way. From the first instant he'd set eyes on Megan, he'd wanted her more than he'd ever wanted any other woman. At first, that attraction had been purely sexual, but it had quickly involved other parts of him, parts he hadn't even been aware had existed before then. She'd touched him in ways no other woman ever had, making him give more of himself to her—and making him want her, in turn, to give more of herself—than he'd given to any other woman he'd ever known. And he'd *told* her that.

He admired everything about her—her fire, her intensity, her characteristic way of approaching everything as if it were a challenge. What made it even more impressive was that it wasn't just high hopes, either; by every indication, she was perfectly capable of accomplishing anything she set out to do, whether it was finding some vital component of an ancient plumbing system, making her way through a combat zone without hysterics, or taking on *him* with a fearlessness most of his adversaries—and plenty of his colleagues—couldn't match. He'd told her that, too.

While he'd always suspected Megan's audacity had been a cover for something, he'd never guessed it could be anything like the insecurities she'd admitted to the night before. Rather than making him think any less of her, they had only made him admire her more. Just because "too tall and skinny for any man to want" was the most preposterous notion *he'd* ever heard didn't mean it hadn't been as real to her as his . . . problem . . . with caves was to him, and she'd handled it a lot better, never letting it defeat her. He wished he'd known. When he hadn't been able to find her after spring break, it had torn him up for months, and it had been even worse after both Nicaragua and Paris. This time, he could already imagine how bad it would be, and he didn't think he could stand to see those predictions realized. He'd even told her that.

So then, what did that damn woman want from him, anyway? His last drop of blood?

THAT NIGHT, AFTER enduring a dinner so grimly silent, open combat would have been welcome relief, Alex pulled Matt aside and asked him how the expedition crew contacted Niko when they wanted to fly over to the mainland. He didn't mention Megan, but then, he didn't have to. Instead, he reminded Matt that he had a job back in Washington, and he ought to get back to it. Mountains of Agency paperwork, including a debriefing on his trip to Zoman, a replacement muffler for his Ford Ranger pickup, and heightened tensions in Central America were all cited in the same breath, as if they, either singly or collectively, had been responsible for his decision.

Rather than directing him to the shortwave radio and then bidding him farewell, Matt told Alex he should consider staying on the island a while longer. He didn't mention Megan, but then, he didn't have to. Instead, he reminded Alex that this was his first real vacation in three years and he ought to take advantage of it while he could. Scuba diving in crystal-clear waters, the Late Archaic shrine they were bound to unearth at any moment, and a tan that would make him the envy of everyone in Washington were all cited in the same breath, as if they, either separately or in some combination, could persuade him to stay.

They almost worked. Certain that Alex really *wanted* to be convinced and only needed another little nudge, Matt appealed to Gus, knowing the cook would sympathize with his campaign and perhaps provide a constructive suggestion or two. Gus grinned and promised to handle the matter, if Matt left it up to him and simply followed his lead.

Almost at once, Matt was left wondering what Gus had been thinking of when he'd said he could handle the problem. As far as that went, he wondered what *he'd* been thinking when he'd turned it over to Gus. But then, how could he have foreseen that Gus's strategic contribution would be the village's festival the following week in honor of Saint Eramios, patron saint of Mediterranean seamen? Frankly, he'd expected something that would be more appealing to Alex—a sudden shortage of hot peppers and eggplant, or a temporary switch to instant coffee, at least.

Matt couldn't help noting that Alex appeared to be equally *under*whelmed by the prospect of attending a religious festival. Since he'd been the one who had dragged Gus into the fray, Matt felt obliged to lend a hand. Together, they struggled to assure Alex that the festival was a peculiar blend of religious homage and pagan rite, all rolled up into one frenzied drunken brawl, much the same as Rio de Janeiro's Carnival or New Orleans's Mardi Gras.

"Every one of the islands has one or two of them each year," Matt told him, speaking with some authority and, he hoped, some semblance of credibility. "I was at the festival on Crete a few years ago, and, trust me, even though they're all supposed to be for saints, religion doesn't have a lot to do with it."

"Singing and dancing and eating and so much drinking..." Gus added eagerly, his eyes glittering. "And every year, nine months later, so many new babies..."

Laughing, Alex held his hands up in surrender. "All right, all right... I'll stay until after that."

STAYING ON HIMEROS didn't mean Alex got to see much more of Megan. Though they'd spent the largest part of the past fifteen years living separate lives on different continents, they had never, Alex thought, seemed farther apart than they did while they were inhabiting

the same tiny island—mainly because Megan was doing her best to stay as far away from him as she could.

And Megan's best was truly a phenomenon to behold. Like an overcautious tourist who'd read one-too-
many State Department bulletins on terrorism, she
seemed determined to give a wide berth to any man
with a heavy accent and one bomb-size piece of luggage. All right, so he *did* still have a good portion of
that drawl, after more than ten years in the North—
which D.C. was, as any good Texan could attest—and
there *was* that pistol in his backpack, but he hadn't
thought about killing her in days. He only tended to
think along those lines when she was insulting or antagonizing him, and she hadn't been doing either of
those things.

Insulting or antagonizing him would have meant
speaking to him, and Megan hadn't said a word to him
since their blowout in the market. She hadn't looked at
him. She hadn't acknowledged his presence in any
fashion, not even when they were all sitting around the
dinner table and the other members of the expedition
were including him in the conversation in a way that
should have made it impossible for her to ignore him.
She ignored him very well. That damned woman knew
how to nurse a grudge better than anyone *he'd* ever
known.

Given the unfriendly conditions on that front, Alex
found himself with plenty of spare time on his hands,
so that any and all suggestions for time-consuming activities were desperately appreciated.

He went scuba diving, exploring the shipwreck Matt
had told him about. While it wasn't an *ancient* relic, but
merely a Venetian merchant ship from the Renais-
sance, it was old enough to be interesting, and he man-

aged to bring some coins and a necklace back up with
him. Even if he couldn't keep them without risking a
stay in a Greek jail and the expedition's diving permit,
it was nearly as good as finding buried treasure.

He went out with the local fishermen, each of them
apparently related to Spiro in at least three different
ways, and helped to haul in the heavy nets with their
catch. While the work was arduous and extremely
smelly, there was a good, honest simplicity about it that
reminded him of working on his father's ranch. It also
exhausted him enough to sleep at night without lying
awake for hours first, alternately thinking about how
close Megan actually was and how much distance she'd
put between them.

Matt coerced him into helping with the dig, telling
him they needed every extra hand available for the last
hard push toward the shrine—or to where they believed it ought to be. What Matt neglected to tell him
was that his lack of experience limited him to the
thankless-but-necessary task of "leveling off" the areas
the archaeologists had already probed and pronounced useless, before turning them over to the pro-
fessionals again. In a nutshell, it was ditchdigging.

Tedious beyond imagining, it *should* have exhausted him as much as working on the fishing boats
did. Instead, he found that spending the entire day at
arm's length from Megan kept him awake most of the
night. It was also close enough for him to observe the
Greek diggers ogling Megan's legs whenever she swung
down into or boosted herself up out of the excavation
pit. She never appeared to notice, and he wanted to
point it out to her, almost as much as he wanted to
throttle every last one of them for the fantasies he *knew*
all that leering indicated.

What stuck in Alex's craw most was that, for a woman who was essentially oblivious to her own desirability, Megan had an affinity for encouraging male interest. Casual displays of affection came naturally to her, and she never gave a thought to the fact that the smiles and hugs she dispensed with such lavish abandon to everyone, it seemed, but him, were bound to provoke somebody, sooner or later, into thinking she was being something more than friendly. He wanted to point *that* out to her, too.

Because Alex was watching the workmen watch Megan as she inspected the latest screen box of soil to come out of the pit, he didn't notice the chunk of rock he'd uncovered until he jammed his shovel right into it with a force that sent shock waves up his arms. It didn't budge, even when he turned the shovel blade-down and poked at it in an attempt to lever it out. Whatever it was, it went well below the four-foot, six-inch depth he was leveling down to. Laying his shovel aside and crouching down for a closer look, Alex peered at the exposed stone for a moment before realizing that, like the arrowheads he'd collected on his father's ranch, it was finished. In a word, *manmade.*

Coming to his feet, he called out to Matt, though he kept his excitement in check, telling himself that if he was dead wrong about what he thought he was seeing and it was only another odd geological formation, everyone working on the dig didn't need to know about it.

Alex could have yelled his head off, as it turned out. He knew it the instant that Matt looked down at the rock and let his breath slowly trail out in one word. "Jesus."

"Is that what I think it is?" Alex asked quietly.

"Who was checking this section, anyway?"

"Helmut."

"Figures." Matt shook his head and sighed. "He hasn't had ten minutes' sleep in the last week."

"I know." So did everyone else in camp, since the intervals of silence from that tent had been few and far between. "Since I found it, does that mean they're gonna name it after me?"

"Only if you intend to pick up the tab for the expedition." Matt grinned. "You know, most men settle for flowers or candy when they've got a woman mad at them."

"Yeah, but then, most women aren't Megan." Alex returned the smile wryly, thinking she'd probably appreciate some ancient piece of plumbing more, and wondering if a shrine would suffice to get him back in her good graces.

It didn't. While Megan was just as thrilled by the shrine's discovery as everyone else on the crew, the rest were a lot more generous in their acknowledgement of *his* role in its unearthing. If the congratulations she offered him had been any more meager or grudging, Alex wasn't sure he'd have recognized them as such.

His disappointment at Megan's less-than-rhapsodic response tarnished both his pride in his find and his enjoyment of the celebration at camp that followed. Although Gus pulled out all the stops for an elaborate feast offering every Greek delicacy imaginable, Alex barely picked at his food. The fact that Gus had gone heavy on the eggplant in the moussaka had nothing to do with his lack of appetite.

No one else seemed to notice that the man of the hour wasn't savoring either the meal or his moment of glory. They were all having too much fun, eating and drinking and laughing and talking in a half-dozen different languages at once. Though everything ended up in English or Spanish sooner or later, Alex didn't much care by that point. He felt oddly detached from it all, as if he were on the outside looking in.

For the first time in his memory, being on the outside bothered Alex. He didn't simply want to be part of the group, either; he wanted something more—something so alien and elusive, he couldn't even say what it was. And his inability to define it bothered him almost as much as the feeling itself. To a lesser degree, the feeling had been hovering over him since his arrival on Himeros. It wasn't constant, but cropped up at intervals since it was touched off by little, otherwise insignificant, things.

Things like the sight of Helmut and Renata, walking together and holding hands, stopping occasionally to kiss or exchange a private word. The small touches and gestures that affirmed that Ian and Jean-Claude—and, to his astonishment, Spiro and Irina—were also lovers. And, while it wasn't the same, since their motivation was clearly affection rather than passion, the signs of the strong bond that still existed between Matt and Megan.

It was Matt, of all people, who identified the feeling for Alex some time later, after everyone else had headed off to their tents for the night. With Megan not speaking to him, Alex and Matt had gotten to be good friends during the week, though it didn't seem either possible or logical that it had happened, and they'd spent every evening drinking a few beers and talking after the others went off to pursue their own interests.

"Almost all the Greek islands' names mean something, you know," Matt remarked in an offhand manner before taking another sip of his beer.

Though the comment didn't have anything to do with the topic they'd been discussing, Alex asked, just as casually, "This one mean anything special?"

"You know who Cupid is, don't you?"

"Valentine's Day? Little guy with wings?"

Matt chuckled and nodded. "Yeah. His Greek name is Eros, and he was Aphrodite's son and one of her helpers. Anyway, there were a bunch of these little guys with wings, and each of them was supposed to be in charge of a different aspect of love. Eros had 'erotic,' which is where the word came from, and Himeros . . . he was the one in charge of 'yearning.'"

"Yearning?" Alex echoed blankly.

"Yeah, *yearning*. You know, wanting something you can't have. Wanting it so bad it hurts."

Although Matt had changed the subject and gone on to other, less sensitive subjects, the word, and Matt's description of what it meant, returned to Alex some time later, when he was alone.

*Yearning. Wanting something you can't have. Wanting it so bad it hurts.*

That pretty much summed up the way he felt about Megan. He wanted her, he couldn't have her, and it hurt. And it was a kind of love, Matt said. Maybe it was. He couldn't say for sure.

Not that it mattered, Alex finally concluded, pushing aside all contemplation of that pointless subject and telling himself that that was the last of it. Defining the word wouldn't do him a damned bit of good, because it wasn't going to explain what it was that was keeping them apart. Only Megan, and maybe God, could do that.

THE MORNING OF SAINT Eramios's festival, Megan woke with a headache she knew had been provoked by the certainty that Alex intended to leave the island right after the festival, and the mixed feelings that knowledge engendered. She was grateful she wouldn't have to see him anymore, wouldn't have to contend with her hopes that he might change, wouldn't have to worry about how she was going to recover once he'd gone. At the same time, to her utter shame, she dreaded his departure, and for all of the same reasons she wanted him to leave. As long as he was still there, there was always a chance that something might happen to change the things that kept them apart.

*Yeah. Sure. Right.*

The likelihood that Alex was going to change at the ripe old age of thirty-seven was right up there with the possibility that aliens from somewhere in the next galaxy were going to fly in and tell her exactly where the missing pieces of the frieze around the top of the shrine had fallen when it had been demolished and later replaced by a temple.

Assuring herself that she was only going to have to make it through another day or so before Alex left, Megan dressed in the embroidered cotton dress she'd bought for the festival; she'd finally relented at Renata's dogmatic and characteristically German insistence that they both had to wear traditional dress, despite their blondness and height, which made them stand out like a pair of sore thumbs among the dark and diminutive Greek women. When she arrived at the cook tent, her sandals dangling from the fingers of one hand, the others were all seated at the breakfast table, the men in jeans or shorts and Renata wearing the dress that was a great deal like hers. Matt was explaining to the others what Gus had told him about the holiday.

"You've heard of Saint Elmo? Same guy, with a Greek name."

"Did he do anything besides make fire?" Ian quipped and, after the remark had been translated into as many languages as necessary, everyone at the table finally laughed.

"It's only named for him," Matt retorted, "because he's the guardian of Mediterranean seamen."

"As opposed to non-Mediterranean sperm?" Ian asked, his eyes wide with a false innocence everyone recognized.

"Sea men. Men of the sea," Matt corrected slowly and patiently.

"Then what *did* he do?" Alex asked.

"He was a bishop," Megan offered helpfully. "At the end of the third century."

Alex turned to look at her. She was wearing a dress that looked so soft and sheer, he had to grip his thighs with his fingers to keep himself from reaching out and touching it. While the bodice was loose, it suggested the swell of her breasts, and the full skirt swirled around her legs, alternately clinging and flowing when she moved. She looked beautiful in it, so feminine and gentle, he almost changed his mind about staying on the island after the festival, for however long it took him to convince her that whatever it was that stood between them didn't matter.

"They disemboweled him and hoisted his intestines on the winch of a ship," Megan finished bluntly.

Alex had a pretty good idea how he'd felt. Seeing Megan like this, wanting her and knowing he couldn't touch her, gave him much the same feeling. This yearning stuff wasn't easy on the system.

"Before or after he was dead?" Ian persisted, still morbidly fascinated with the subject.

"Got me. I forget." Megan shrugged, and the neckline of her dress slid off one shoulder, revealing that she wasn't wearing a bra, or at least not one with straps. Alex wanted to reach out and readjust the neckline so no one could see her bare shoulder. That Ian had no interest in Megan's or, for that matter, any female shoulder, didn't ease that compulsion.

"The diggers wanted to make sure they got to the village in time for church," Matt volunteered, changing the subject. Secretly, he suspected their motivation had a lot more to do with their desire not to miss a single drop of the liquor that would start to flow immediately after Father Theodouris said "Amen." "So I shuttled them in already and we're all that's left. It'll be a tight fit, but we can take the Land Rover in one trip if we double up."

They could, though, as Matt had told them, it was a tight fit. He was driving, so Ian and Jean-Claude squeezed together in the other front seat and Renata sat on Helmut's lap in the back, leaving only Alex and Megan for the other half of the back seat. They stood and looked at each other warily for several moments before Matt interjected, "One of you's gonna have to sit on the other's lap. Which way it goes is entirely up to you."

Nobody moved.

"Do I have to toss a coin?" Matt snapped, exasperated by both of them. In spite of his best efforts, he hadn't made a bit of progress in getting the two to-gether in the past week. Which of them was being more stubborn and obtuse was anybody's guess. "Alex, get in."

Having no real objections to the seating arrange-ments, Alex did as he was told. Megan, however, propped her fists on her hips and refused to budge.

"You going along, Meggie?" Matt asked. "In."

"Something wrong with the scooter? Alex can take that." The last thing she wanted to do was sit on Alex's lap, because she knew that being there would remind her that that was really where she wanted to be.

"Gus took it this morning. Any more questions?" He didn't give her a chance, and just nodded. "Good. That's settled, then. Catch, Alex." With that little warning, he grabbed Megan at the waist, lifted her up, and tossed her over the side of the Land Rover into Al-ex's lap.

While Alex's reflexes were good enough to keep Me-gan from falling onto the floor or out of the Land Rover, they weren't good enough to prevent her from being draped all over him in an indecorous sprawl. She was facedown, almost folded in half across his lap, with her head hanging down toward the floorboard and her skirt flapping up around her thighs just below the curve of her buttocks. Because one arm had thrust between his legs when she'd landed, her shoulder was wedged into the V of his crotch, a location that became downright hazardous once she recovered from her initial surprise and started to wriggle, trying to get herself free and upright.

"Megan . . ." he began in a strained voice as he tried to hold her still. It was a futile effort. If anything, she struggled more. "Megan... Dammit, Megan! Stop that right now!"

He gave a moment's thought to swatting her on her rear, which was almost too tempting to resist; he didn't dare, however, because she was too well-situated for retaliation. Left with few alternatives, he hooked one hand under her knee, took hold of her upper arm with the other, and flipped her over onto her back. While her bottom touched down with a little more velocity—and thus force—than he'd intended, on the whole, the situation was greatly improved, since he was no longer in immediate danger of emasculation. What she might do to him later was another question altogether; it was all too apparent that she was far from pleased.

With an angry squawk, she reached for the roll bar, curled her fingers around it, and hauled herself up. Before she could steady herself, Matt let out the clutch and the Land Rover lurched forward with a jerk that propelled her, hip-first, against Alex's vulnerable lap. Even as he gulped and tears of pain sprang up in his eyes, his arms closed around her waist automatically. At the same time that he was trying to keep her from falling out, he was also trying to protect his manhood. Given her lack of cooperation, it wasn't an easy task.

"Keep your hands to yourself, would you?" she hissed under her breath as she retained her tenuous hold on the roll bar and struggled to pull herself up and out, away from him. All she accomplished, however, was to increase the pressure of her hip against him.

"You're not the one in danger here," he muttered, sliding his hands down to her hips, cupping her bottom with one hand, and lifting her. "Watch that bony hip of yours!"

"Bony?" She twisted to confront him, fire in her eyes.

While the maneuver eased the pressure on his groin, it also compressed her breast against the side of his face. The yielding plumpness affirmed that she wore no bra at all, either with or without straps. A new pressure, one with an internal rather than an external cause, afflicted his groin at the discovery. He groaned as her distinctive feminine scent infiltrated and congested his senses, brain, and points farther south. He wanted to turn his face, bury it between the lush mounds of her breasts, and breathe in the fragrance. Instead he growled, so quietly no one but Megan could hear it, "If you don't get your nipple out of my mouth, I'm gonna think you aren't mad at me anymore."

With an indignant gasp, she spun away to face forward and curled her fingers over the top of Matt's seat. Alex watched her strain to hold herself rigidly upright as the vehicle rumbled off down the pock-filled road. She succeeded admirably, hanging on by her fingernails and sheer determination, until a particularly deep rut sent her sliding back again. This time, Alex saw the hazard ahead, and managed to halt the movement before she did him irreparable harm. Before the risky tussle could start up again, he slipped his arms about her waist, tightening them to hold her in place.

Megan gave up and settled in on Alex's lap, resolutely ignoring the sidelong, speculative glances of the others. The concession was prompted by her recognition of Alex's superior strength, the knowledge that the ride to town was brief, and the awareness that if someone fell over the side and fractured a skull, it would be her.

Their arrival in the village couldn't come one moment too soon for Megan. She was desperate to be released from Alex's tight embrace. His arms were around her rib cage just beneath her breasts and rubbing against them—all too frequently, she suspected, for the touches to be anything but deliberate.

While there'd been a time when she would have given anything to feel Alex's strong arms around her, that had been before she'd admitted that there was not, and never would be, any tenderness or human caring in his embrace. Any hope she'd had that he might change had been firmly trounced by the safe distance he'd kept between them since that night on the beach the week before. And that was just a more prominent variety of the distance he'd always kept between them. Not even the swell of his erection nudging her backside could support her hope that it could be otherwise. She knew as well as anyone that Alex wasn't a cuddler, either before or after sex; cuddling was, after all, too much like tenderness.

It was something she had to keep repeating to herself, because that stern reminder was the only thing keeping her from relaxing in his arms and melting back against him in a boneless, malleable heap.

For Alex, Megan's presence on his lap was no triumph at all, and only the most superficial kind of pleasure. It was apparent she not only wasn't there willingly, she was there under duress. Her spine was as stiff and straight as an iron rod. He stroked and kneaded the rigid muscles that encased her rib cage, but they refused to yield to his touch.

He glanced sideways at Helmut and Renata. Helmut's arms, like Alex's, were wrapped around the woman on his lap, but the similarity ended there. Renata was snuggling against him, as if she couldn't get close enough. As he nuzzled the side of her throat, she rubbed her cheek against the side of his face and her fingers opened and closed against his thigh. She looked like a kitten being petted, almost purring with contentment.

Megan, on the other hand, looked as if she were getting ready to growl and scratch and bite. He remembered, all too well, when those reactions had been generated by passion instead of hostility. His body responded to the memory, his hand closed reflexively around the underside of her breast, and he felt his arousal rise to the next degree of readiness, in spite of his silent admonition to it not to get too excited, because getting hard was, under the circumstances, a pure waste of energy.

Biting back the tortured groan that rose in his throat and demanded to be released, he assured himself it wouldn't be much longer before they were in town and Megan was off his lap. Beyond that, it wouldn't even be much longer before he was off Himeros and away from Megan for good. And this time, it *would* be for good. He wasn't going to go after Megan again. Not even if Frank threatened him with charges of insubordination. Not even if there wasn't another agent available anywhere in the world. Not even if Megan was being held prisoner by sadistic white-slaving terrorists with nuclear devices.

*Yeah. Sure. Right.*

# 11

THE FESTIVAL FOR SAINT Eramios was every bit as rowdy as Matt and Gus had said it would be. Once the mass was over so was the entire religious portion of the festivities, letting the villagers, diggers and tourists begin to celebrate.

There was music everywhere in a boisterous composite of native Greek songs, bawdy fishing chanteys, and current and old American hits, inspiring impromptu sing-alongs and dancing that took control of the streets. The singers and dancers enthusiastically ignored any national or social distinctions between either the various songs or their partners. The jet-setters who had come in off their yachts sang and danced to accordion and balalaika music with the locals. Matt sang and danced to Aerosmith's "Walk This Way" with Irina, and Megan sang and danced to everything and with everyone—Gus, Spiro, the diggers, the fishermen, and the men from the yachts.

There was food, too, mountains of it, as well as drink. Fish, in honor of Saint Eramios, was the featured fare of the day, cooked in every possible variety and variation. There were also grilled lamb and chicken, rice and eggplant dishes, stuffed grapevine leaves, and a wide variety of sweets, from baklava to honey-soaked farina cake. Bottles of retsina, the potent Greek wine, ouzo, the native anise liqueur with a devastating kick, and beer were all passed around and consumed like water.

Even before noon, everyone, including the village priest, Father Theodouris, had progressed well beyond tipsy to unruly. By an hour after the sun had passed its zenith, he and Gus were officiating at an impromptu craps game. The priest's full black cassock swirled around him, his hat was slightly askew and his long beard twitched, as he knelt in the dusty street and squinted at the dice, laboriously counting the dots and declaring the winner.

Only Alex stood on the sidelines, Megan noted, watching the revelry with a faintly disapproving expression on his face and a glass of ouzo, milky white with the addition of water, in his hand. Both Irina's attempts to get him to dance and Spiro's and Gus's invitation to join in the craps game had been rebuffed, politely enough, but just as adamantly. Knowing he'd stayed specifically for the festival, Megan couldn't understand why he wouldn't celebrate with the rest of them; he might as well have left a week earlier, because he didn't look as if he were having a good time. *Maybe,* she thought, taking a swig from a bottle of retsina offered by her current dancing partner, *he doesn't know how.* That wouldn't surprise her at all.

Alex scowled as he watched Megan take a swig from a bottle offered by one of the men from the yachts and then hand it back with a flirtatious smile. Her cheeks were flushed, her hair mussed, and the shoulder of her dress had slipped down on her upper arm again. She looked as if she'd just gotten out of bed after a satisfying tumble, the only thing contradicting that impression was that she hadn't been out of Alex's sight for a single instant. From the looks of it, the well-tanned yachtsman had every intention of ending up there. The other men were just the same, swarming around Megan like bees around honey, until he wanted to claim her with a roar that she was *his* honey and they couldn't have her.

She wasn't, though. She wasn't even speaking to him, last time he checked.

Alex's brooding continued until it was interrupted by Matt, who approached him with a bottle of beer in each hand. Holding one out to Alex, he said, "You keep drinking that rotgut, it's gonna kill you." A motion of his chin indicated the glass of ouzo Alex had been sipping at—just occasionally, at first, and then more often, as the day had gone on. "You know Gus makes that stuff himself, don't you?"

Alex promptly abandoned the glass on a little stone wall behind him and took the bottle of beer. "No, I didn't, as a matter of fact."

"*Much* more dangerous than any white lightning we've got back in the States. Might make you blind." Matt tipped his bottle and took a long pull of beer. "You look like you wanna kill someone. Anybody I know?"

"Depends," Alex admitted with a grimace. "You know the guy with the Riviera tan?"

"One of the yacht rats," Matt replied with a glance at Megan's partner. "More time and money than they know what to do with."

Alex nodded in sullen understanding.

"You don't really think she'd be interested in that guy, do you? He's a parasite. Meg's smarter than that." After another sip, he added, in a voice that reflected some doubt, "At least, I think she is."

Every muscle in Alex's body clenched as he thought about Megan and the yachtsman together, and got an all-too-vivid mental picture of the scene, complete with sweat-dampened naked bodies, rumpled sheets, and the sounds of passion.

While Alex's face remained as impassive as always, some part of what he was thinking was so strong, it was reflected in his eyes. Matt was now familiar enough with Alex and his limited emotional repertoire to recognize and sympathize with the sentiment. All he could do, however, was provide Alex with another shove in the right direction. "You know, Alex, if you just give up, you can't possibly win. Somebody else's gonna get her. Somebody who tried."

For the rest of the afternoon, Matt wondered if Alex had heard a word he'd said, let alone paid any attention. The man continued to watch Megan, with a hungry expression on his face, as she danced with every male there between the ages of seven and seventy. Matt also noticed that, in spite of her demand as a partner, Megan looked in Alex's direction every chance she got—covertly, to be sure, but with an expression on her face that was virtually identical to his. He wished there was something he could do to help, but he knew no one except Megan and Alex could correct what was wrong between them.

As darkness fell over the island, the revelry continued into the night, escalating as the activities that had been scattered all over town converged in the village square, which was gaily lit by bonfires and swags of colored lights. Tables and chairs were situated all around the dance floor so people too exhausted to move could rest until they got their second wind. When Alex followed Megan and her current partner there, he saw the others from the expedition—Ian and Jean-Claude, Helmut and Renata, Matt, and Gus—all sitting at one of the tables together. He dragged a chair over from one of the other tables to join them.

Even before Alex's bottom hit the seat of his chair, Gus glared at him with a thunderous expression on his face and, in a voice loud enough to be heard over the vintage disco music, demanded, "Why you let Megan dance with all those other men? *You* should dance with her!"

As if the thought hadn't crossed his mind a thousand times already, Alex reflected miserably. He would have asked her to dance, if she hadn't jumped out of the Land Rover and scurried halfway across town the moment Matt had stopped the vehicle. He didn't need to be hit over the head to get the message that she wanted nothing more to do with him. Ever. And, this time, he believed it. Noting the way the firelight shone through Megan's skirt, silhouetting her legs so everyone there could see them, he shook his head and said, in a guarded voice, "I don't dance."

Gus made a disgusted noise and added a Greek curse that required no translation before returning to English. "At festival of Saint Eramios, everybody dance!"

Ian and Jean-Claude, sitting side by side, Ian with his arm draped across the back of the Frenchman's chair, both looked to Gus for verification of that claim. Matt, next to Gus, shook his head and muttered under his breath, "I don't think they're either open-minded or drunk enough for that yet."

"Maybe later?" Ian asked hopefully.

"Not in this lifetime." Before Matt could expound upon that assertion, Irina's nineteen-year-old niece, visiting from the nearby island of Santorini, approached the table and asked him to dance. Though he'd seen enough of a family resemblance to make the girl a dubious prospect over the long term, she was young and pretty now, and he accepted.

As he left the table with his arm around her waist, he heard Gus continue to badger Alex. He silently wished them both luck, and went out onto the floor.

"Well, if you won't dance with Megan, you should dance with someone, like she does," Gus went on, undeterred. "Renata will dance with you."

"Gus, you..."

Before Alex could finish his protest, Gus called her name. The German woman, seated on Helmut's lap with his arm around her waist, looked up in response. "*Ja?*"

"Alex wants to dance. You dance with him?"

She looked to Ian for translation and he provided it. After a brief German discussion of the matter—Helmut clearly didn't want Renata dancing with anybody else, a sentiment Alex could appreciate—Renata said something that, apparently, settled the issue, rose, and held out her hand. Since Alex couldn't explain anything to her without a translator, and Gus wouldn't take any excuses, Alex got up, took her hand, and followed her out into the crowd.

The acting disc jockey, one of the local fishermen, changed to the next record. Like most of the songs he'd been playing, it was another from Alex's college days, this time a slow one—Orleans' "Dance With Me." As he put his arms around Renata and they began to move to the music, Alex looked about for Megan, wondering who she was dancing with.

"Alex..." Renata began. She stopped abruptly, obviously frustrated. Whether it was that he kept looking over first one of her shoulders and then the other or that her limited English was inadequate for her purposes was open to question.

"Yes?" His head snapped forward and he looked down at her.

"*Ich sehe Megan mit dem Priester tanzt.*"

The only word Alex understood was "Megan." It was enough to pique his interest, since he no longer saw her anywhere. Had she gone off with one of her partners? If so, who? Where? And why? He gaped down at the woman, hoping she would miraculously acquire an English vocabulary. Failing that, he hoped he'd suddenly develop the ability to understand German. It didn't matter that both aspirations were irrational.

"*Megan tanzt mit dem Priester,*" Renata repeated, more slowly and clearly, as if that would enable Alex to understand her. It made him think of the old jokes about non-Spanish-speaking Texans who went south of the border and tried the same tactic with the Mexicans, with a similar lack of success.

At last, Renata gripped his shoulders, steering him around so he was facing in the direction she'd been facing before the move. He saw Megan at once and, just as quickly, realized what *Priester* meant. *Priest.* She was dancing with Father Theodouris. Alex breathed a sigh of profound relief, looked down at Renata, and smiled, communicating his comprehension as he repeated her identification. "*Priester.*"

Smiling back, Renata nodded. "*Ist harmlos.*"

Alex didn't need a translator to recognize the meaning of that word. Father Theodouris was in his sixties and as completely harmless as if Greek Orthodox priests had been sworn to celibacy like their Roman Catholic counterparts. The only danger Megan was in at the moment was that the priest, who had passed three sheets to the wind hours earlier, might fall on her. While he was considerably shorter than she was, he was twice her weight.

The record changed, to Billy Joel's "She's Always a Woman," and Renata and Alex, deciding tacitly and simultaneously that they'd fulfilled Gus's mandate and more dancing would only annoy Helmut, went back to the table. Renata returned to her seat on Helmut's lap and, as she began to make peace with him in whispers and kisses, Alex took a sip of his beer and reclaimed his chair. As he did, he looked to Gus to confirm that he'd done as ordered. He'd expected to see approval on Gus's face; instead, all he saw was an expression of extreme consternation as the man looked, not at Alex, but out onto the dance floor. Turning, Alex followed his gaze and his jaw clenched.

Megan was dancing with Niko, the helicopter pilot whose very long last name, Alex remembered, began with a *P.* The fact that she'd danced with every other male on the island did absolutely nothing to pacify Alex. Niko wasn't a parasite like the yacht rat. He wasn't indifferent to Megan, as Matt was. He wasn't harmless like Father Theodouris. He wasn't like any of the other fishermen or diggers or tourists she'd been dancing with all day.

Not one of them had raised his head, picked Alex out of the crowd, met his eyes squarely, and then smiled in a manner that conveyed his triumph in no uncertain terms.

*You know, Alex, if you just give up, you can't possibly win. Somebody else's gonna get her. Somebody who tried.*

As Matt's earlier comment came back to him, a furious tremor of reaction began at Alex's jaw and stormed down through his body in percussive waves so forceful, they impaired his vision and thought processes and ravaged his muscle control. When he tried to set his beer bottle on the table, it fell over, and only a quick recovery by Gus kept it from rolling to the ground. While he didn't acknowledge the save, he ground out at Gus, "You still have the key to the bike?"

Gus nodded, though Alex didn't see it. "Here." Producing the key, the cook pressed it into his hand, which closed around it even as he started out onto the dance floor toward Megan and Niko, ruthlessly elbowing aside the other dancers. A surge of primitive possessiveness shot through Alex, so strong he couldn't mistake it for anything else. No matter what had happened in the fifteen years since the first and last time they had made love—their separation, her marriage to Matt, and her current fury with him—the fact remained that Megan was his, and Niko couldn't have her.

While Megan didn't see Alex's approach, Niko did, and his arms tightened, pulling her against him in a tight embrace. The move, and his resulting proximity, startled her, because he'd never shown any romantic interest in her before. For one thing, Niko liked his women shorter than he was, which she wasn't, not by a long shot.

With a weary sigh, she wondered whether she ought to say something. A moment later, positive his sudden amorousness was nothing more than the unfortunate consequence of all he'd had to drink, she decided not to bother. Niko was so drunk, she could have been any warm body—quite literally. When he'd asked her to dance, his slurred speech and unsteadiness had told her he'd been imbibing as liberally as anyone else on the island. If he was up to the grappling stage, she guessed he had another ten minutes, tops, before he passed out. The perception transferred her immediate concern from Niko's groping to getting him to a chair before she had to catch him, a task she wasn't prepared to handle after propping up Father Theodouris.

Putting her arm around him, she turned and began to navigate him in the general direction of the tables. Before she could get him there, however, another man's arm hooked her around the torso just below her ribs, dragging her back against a hard masculine body with contours so familiar, she didn't need to hear the voice behind her to identify him. Actually, it was the voice itself that confused her. It was an unfamiliar angry snarl she'd never heard before and didn't recognize.

"You get your hands off her and keep 'em off." Alex jerked Megan against his body, the force knocking her breath out of her lungs and pulling her up off her feet like a rag doll. "She's mine, you hear? *Mine.*"

Her head whipped around and she gaped up at Alex, her mouth dropping open with shock at both his blunt declaration and his feral expression. He wasn't just angry; he was positively livid in a manner she would never have believed possible if she wasn't seeing it with her own eyes.

"Dammit, you don't speak English, so you can't understand. Tell him, Megan." He gave her ribs a quick squeeze and released them, not painfully, but in an effort to prompt her. "Tell him you're mine."

Megan didn't say anything; the revelation of Alex's savagely primitive jealousy rendered her utterly speechless. She couldn't muster a single word, not even in English, let alone remember how to translate what he was saying into Greek.

When she didn't say anything, he cursed again, using a word she knew Niko would recognize from his contact with American servicemen, and then he looked down at her, his green eyes filled with something that looked suspiciously like anguish. "Was I wrong, Megan? Tell me. Please, God, tell me."

Tears welled in her eyes at his choked demand. Her chest heaved as she drew a deep quivering breath into her lungs, let it out again, and then shook her head emphatically. She swallowed once, tried to speak, and failed.

In an explicit demonstration of what neither of them could put into words that Niko could understand, Alex roughly turned Megan in his arms, hauled her up against him, and lowered his mouth to hers in a kiss that was greedy and ruthlessly possessive. It was also the sweetest kiss Megan had ever had and revealed a raw passion in Alex that was more than physical desire. It was sheer emotion, the likes of which she had never seen him display, genuine human need, and something else—something her mind was afraid to classify after all the previous evidence that Alex didn't have it in him.

Megan stopped thinking logically and let the unconscious portion of her mind, the part that believed, take command of her body, allowing her to respond with none of the suspicions or reservations that had haunted her and held her back the week before. She opened her arms, lifting them to encircle Alex's neck as she arched her body against his. She opened her mouth, wordlessly enticing his questing tongue inside and then whimpering when it touched hers. And she opened her heart, hoping his newfound emotions would allow him to accept it and do the same.

Even as he deepened his kiss, clung more tightly to Megan, and acknowledged the rightness of what he was doing, the part of Alex's brain that had governed his behavior his whole life was both astounded and appalled by this reversion to his primitive roots. He barely recognized himself as this possessive, jealous male, claiming his mate in a primordial manner that had existed virtually unchanged for tens of thousands of years. At the same time that it was intended to deter any and all challengers for his woman, it was meant to tell her, in no uncertain terms, to whom she belonged.

Alex was totally out of control. He knew it and, in spite of the yammering from his common sense and a lifetime's worth of admonitions to maintain his self-control, the knowledge didn't particularly trouble him. By all appearances, it didn't bother Megan, either. To say the very least, she wasn't fighting him anymore. She was melting in his arms, accepting him, apparently trusting him and believing him as she never had before. While he couldn't put a name to the feelings her response generated, he reveled in them, letting them engulf him until they blocked out everything else but the two of them. He didn't hear the music or the people, didn't see the twinkling lights or bonfires, didn't smell the pungent aromas of fish and liquor. His senses were too filled with Megan for him to be aware of anything else.

Although the feeling was new and unknown and more unnerving than a hundred caves, Alex wanted more. He wanted it all, and it didn't matter that he wasn't quite sure what "all" was or how to get it. He had a pretty good idea Megan knew. It was what she wanted from him, too; it was what she'd been trying to tell him all along. The only thing he knew for sure was that, whatever it was, it was more than sex. A lot more.

He lifted his head, pulling his mouth away from hers, and opened his eyes. A moment later, Megan's eyes opened, too, gazing into his with a glimmer that spoke, simultaneously, of both wonderment and triumph. A single tear trickled down her cheek and he lifted his hands, cupped her face, and brushed it away with his thumb as a sharp pang penetrated his chest.

"Don't cry, Megan," he whispered, the sound barely audible over the music.

"I'm not crying," she said with a sniff.

"Liar," he softly accused with a low chuckle that took the venom out of the charge.

"You feel it, too, don't you? You finally understand?"

"I feel it, but I don't understand it. I don't know what it is, but I want it." He saw a sudden darkness flicker across her eyes and rapidly added, in a voice that sounded frustrated, even to him, "I'm trying, Megan. Help me out, here."

The darkness fled and was replaced by tenderness. She smiled and lifted one hand to stroke his jaw. "Don't worry about it, Alex. As long as you're trying, I'll help."

"I don't know how . . . ."

"I'll teach you." She rose up onto the balls of her feet and kissed him gently. "But I think we should go back to camp for the first lesson."

Alex raised his head, looked around, and flushed a brilliant scarlet as he suddenly became aware of the huge audience watching them, undeterred by the personal nature of what they were observing. He quickly lowered his head, buried his face next to Megan's ear, and muttered, "So how do we get out of here without completely disgracing ourselves?"

"We just leave?" she proposed innocently, although he knew she was aware of how untenable that suggestion was even before he pressed his hips against hers, demonstrating that he was in no condition to appear in public without her body shielding him. "Maybe not."

"*Definitely* not."

"You could," she said with an ingenuous smile, "always dance with me for a while. Maybe it'll get better."

"Only if you behave yourself." He tightened his arms around her, rested his cheek against her temple, and began to move in time with the music. Since everyone else, including Niko, had vacated the floor as soon as the trouble had started, they were alone. Absorbed in the sensation of Megan's body moving against his, a sensation that wasn't alleviating his condition, he paid no attention to what music was playing until he felt her body begin to shake with silent laughter. "What is it?"

"Listen. 'Last Dance.' Donna Summer. How appropriate."

By the end of the song, Alex had regained enough control over himself for them to leave the dance floor with his dignity reasonably intact, despite the cheers and hooting for another steamy kiss. When they located the scooter, which Gus had stowed in a nearby alley, Alex gave Megan a slow, lingering kiss that promised much more, very soon. Sliding his hands up her ribs and cupping her breasts, he murmured, "All day, I knew you weren't wearing a bra, and it was driving me crazy."

"It was?" The question wasn't doubtful or disbelieving; it was purred in a frankly provocative manner.

"Mmm-hmm," he confirmed with another kiss. "And every time your dress slid off your shoulder . . ."

"Like this?" She shrugged, and it did precisely that.

"Mmm-hmm. I wanted to kiss you there. . . ." He bent his head and touched his open mouth to the curve of her shoulder, downy soft and slightly salty. "I wanted to slide my hand inside, and touch you there. . . ." He lifted his hand, slipped it inside the neckline, and brushed the tips of his fingers over the crest of one breast, damp and rigidly peaked. "I see I'm not the only thing that's hard around here." He dropped a quick kiss on her mouth before he moved away from her, toward the scooter. "What do you say we head on back to camp?"

Alex straddled the scooter, started it, and turned to offer Megan his hand so she could mount the bike behind him. Instead of getting on, she just stared at the scooter with a leery expression on her face.

"You don't trust me? The woman who oughta be confined to cars on tracks doesn't trust *my* driving?"

She didn't refute the comment, which was only made in jest, as she could see by the laughter in his eyes. It was so good to see real feeling there, she couldn't bring herself to discourage him, even if the joke was both chauvinistic and at her expense.

"What is it, then, Megan?"

"I'm wearing a skirt," she grumbled.

"So hike it up."

"But . . ." Megan looked over her shoulder, back toward the village square.

"I'll take the back way out of town," Alex assured her. "No one'll see your legs but me. And, trust me, darlin', I *love* your legs."

The words *darlin'* and *love* spoken by Alex in the same sentence were almost too much for Megan to assimilate. Rewarding him, she hauled her skirt up around her upper thighs and climbed on. As she wrapped her arms around his waist, she squeezed him and nuzzled the nape of his neck. "You love my legs, do you?"

"I can't begin to tell you how many fantasies I've had about them in the last fifteen years." After giving the throttle of the machine a sharp turn to keep it from stalling, he lowered his hand to her calf and then slid it up the sleek length of her leg. "Especially the little mole *right there*." Without looking, he unerringly pressed his thumb against the precise location, high on the inside of her thigh.

With a soft groan, Megan retrieved his hand and replaced it on the grip. "Let's get back to camp, Alex. Fast."

It wasn't a request he intended to argue with, not even to break the news that the scooter wasn't capable of moving fast. At least his work on it had escalated its maximum velocity to faster than the speed of sheep. Instead of taking thirty minutes to get back to the compound, as it had the first time he'd ridden it into the village, it only took fifteen.

Because they were the first to return to camp, darkness and silence fell over them as soon as Alex shut off the motor and lights. Megan's arms dropped from their position around his waist and they both sat there for several moments, each waiting for the other to make the first move. Finally, Alex swung his leg over the seat and perched on it sideways between her legs as he turned to her, lifting his hand to cup her cheek. With a low purr of contentment, she rubbed it against his palm.

"You're like a cat," Alex observed. "You like to be touched, don't you?"

"Lesson one, Alex. *Everyone* likes to be touched. Everyone *needs* to be touched." She stroked the hard curve of his chest and his breath caught in his throat, as if affirming the premise. "Scientists say that if babies aren't touched, held, petted, they fail to thrive and they die."

Alex forced himself to nod, though he knew the movement was shaky at best.

"Hold me, Alex," Megan whispered, and he put his arms around her. While their current location meant it wasn't going any further than that at the moment, there was a pleasure in the simple embrace that he'd never really thought about before. Her body was warm and fragile, femininely soft where his was hard, and alluring in a way that wasn't merely sensual, but was sensuous, as well.

He nuzzled her neck and asked in a husky whisper, "Am I ready for lesson two yet?"

# 12

"MMM-HMM." THE ANSWER came from deep in Megan's throat, more a vibration against Alex's lips than a sound.

"Should I bring anything?"

"Mmm-hmm. Your mattress and sleeping bag. We can put them on the ground, like Helmut and Renata do...."

Alex nodded; it hadn't escaped his notice that the cots weren't sturdy. He didn't doubt that the combined weight of two people, particularly two moving people, would probably send them crashing to the ground. While the reminder to bring his sleeping bag and mattress was useful, it wasn't what he'd been asking, however. He opened his mouth, but she stopped him, adding, "And Ian and Jean-Claude . . ."

"You wanna do me a favor, darlin', and not mention them right now? I mean, they're nice enough and all, and I believe in live and let live, but . . ."

"Your Texas is showing," she accused in a teasing voice.

"I certainly hope so." He ran his finger down her nose and across her mouth and she caught it between her lips and held it there, sucking on it. For a moment, he completely forgot what he'd been about to say. He retrieved his finger, dropped a kiss on her mouth, and asked, "I wasn't asking about sleeping bags and mattresses, Megan. Are you on the Pill?"

She groaned. "I went off after the divorce, and since then I haven't needed—"

He stopped her words with another kiss, feeling a surge of emotion he recognized as the same one that had assailed him fifteen years earlier, when he'd discovered she was a virgin. "Don't worry about it."

"But . . ."

"I'll see what I can do," Alex assured her with another quick kiss. "Go on along into your tent, and I'll be there as soon as I can."

Several minutes later, Alex dumped his sleeping bag and mattress outside Megan's tent, pushed aside the flap, and ducked his head to step inside. The tape player, softly playing "Feels Like the First Time," by Foreigner—had she heard it, too, and still remembered?—and a lantern, adjusted to its lowest level, sat on the bare springs of her cot, which had been shoved to the back of the tent. The bedding itself was on the ground, pushed to one side to leave room for his. Megan stood in her bare feet but still had on the embroidered dress; the light filtered through the diaphanous fabric, outlining her legs as plainly as the lights in the town square had. This time, though, it was for him alone. As she turned, smiling gently, and stepped toward him, he swallowed heavily, wanting her and wishing he didn't have to make the admission he knew he couldn't avoid.

"Megan . . ." he began.

Before he could continue, Megan reached out to touch his chest and skimmed her hands down to his waist with a touch that was as light as a breeze. When she found the hard ridge beneath his fly, he groaned and caught her hands. Holding them at a safe distance from his body, he took a deep breath, then tried again. "Megan, I have something to tell you. *Now*, before we start something we might not be able to finish. I don't have anything to protect you."

As if she were a balloon stuck with a pin, Megan deflated visibly, her head and shoulders sagging with disappointment and frustration.

Alex seriously considered going back and checking Matt's gear more thoroughly, despite the guilt and embarrassment his first exploration had provoked. Instead, he gently slid his hands up her arms to her shoulders and said, "Megan, darlin'?"

"Yes?" She lifted her gaze to his. He quickly lowered his head and captured her lips.

"Damn, this is hard," he muttered a moment later, once he released them. "Megan, I know I don't have any right to ask, not after the way I've acted, the things I've said . . . hell, the way I *am*. But I'm trying. I'll keep trying. . . . I meant it when I said you were mine. Not just tonight, but always."

Her eyes went wide with surprise. In spite of it, she nodded and softly asked, "Why, Alex?"

"I can't leave you again, or let you leave, either. Not this time." He blurted out the words, took a deep breath, and then took the plunge. "I want us to stay together, be together. . . ."

Her breath caught in her throat, but she choked out, "Me, too, Alex. But why?"

Damn, the woman was persistent. "I want us to sleep together, make love, make babies. . . ."

She sighed and smiled. It was just like Alex to make lists, instead of simply stating the obvious. If one of them was going to sum it up in its most basic terms, it was evidently going to have to be her. "If you want to take the risk, so do I. I love you, Alex."

For a moment, Alex blinked at her, not believing his ears. She'd spoken so quietly, he was certain he must have misunderstood her. No woman alive, he was sure, could say something like that with such utterly cool certainty, as if she'd been suggesting something as simple as having dinner together. "Could you please repeat that?"

"Do I really need to?" She raised her hands to the front of his shirt and began to undo the buttons one by one, pressing her mouth to the skin beneath as the gap created by the opening moved downward. When she reached the last of his ribs, she stopped and looked up at him with another serene smile. "I want you to be mine, too, not just tonight, but always. I want us to stay together, be together, sleep together, make love, make babies. I want to do all those things because I love you."

He sucked in his breath so sharply it hurt, and lifted his hands to cradle her head. "Is that what love is, Megan?"

Her hair caressed his bare midriff as she nodded.

"It's what I've wanted all along, ever since Florida. I...I didn't know. I never knew...." He sank down onto the mattress, pulling her over him and holding her tight. "Please, Megan, teach me what it means."

There were no more words as she curved her hands around his face and lowered her mouth to his. Only the sounds of passion and surrender broke the silence as she took the initiative, translating the things he'd taught her about sex so long ago into the language of love. Her tongue invaded his mouth, seeking shelter in his warmth, as she tugged his shirt from his jeans, fumbled at the last two buttons, and then scraped it open to bare his chest. With one last kiss and a nip at his beard-roughened jaw, she slid downward, pressing her lips to his chest, licking the skin until she found one nipple, bronze and flat, with a hard bead in the center. As she finessed it with her tongue, his body went rigid, he sucked in his breath, and his hands moved up to cup her head, his fingers lacing through her hair.

It was the sweetest kind of torture for Alex, one he'd imagined for years. There was a tenderness about it, a desire to give, that went beyond the erotic; and, because passivity wasn't in his nature, he wanted to give to her as much as he wanted to take. While one of his hands remained in her hair, stroking her scalp and encouraging her to continue, the other slipped inside her neckline, touching the curve of her breast, stroking the nipple that was as hard as his own. An instant later, the hot rush of breath against his chest verified that the sensation was as potent for her as it was for him. Tangling his fingers more tightly in her hair, he gently lifted her mouth from him and rolled them over so she was beneath him.

Megan watched through narrowed eyes as, straddling her, Alex tugged off his shirt. Her palms tingled, wanting to touch him again, but when she tried to do so, he stopped her, leaning over to restrain her hands against the mattress on either side of her head. He pressed his mouth to hers, thrusting his tongue inside, stroking her until she arched her body up against his, not in protest, but in appeal. It went beyond simple desire to the most elemental kind of need—to genuine compulsion, as if either denial or delay would destroy her. She knew he wanted it, too; she could feel him hard against her lower belly. When he raised himself to an upright position and looked down at her, the smoldering expression in his eyes and the agonized rigidity in his jaw told her, too. This time, she knew they were caused by his struggle for control over his body, not emotions, which were clearly beyond his control.

She looked so beautiful to him, the embodiment of hot feminine passion. Her hair was tousled, her face flushed. Her chest heaved with her breathing, a movement made even more conspicuous and provocative by the way her raised arms lifted her breasts up, pressing her nipples against the soft fabric of her dress. He knew, even without touching her between her thighs, that she was ready for him. Her entire body was vibrating with passion and he could smell the musky scent of it, hot, pungent, and so forcefully arousing he knew neither one of them could wait another moment for release.

As if that fact weren't already apparent to both of them, the feeling of sudden loss they shared when he rocked back onto his heels validated it. At the withdrawal of his weight from her hips and her wrists, Megan scrambled up, propping herself on her elbows as she emitted a wordless cry of objection.

"Don't fret, darlin'," Alex assured her in a low whisper, raising one hand to her lips to capture the sound. He was seated on the mattress between her thighs, his legs spread and draped over hers. "I'm comin' back, just as soon as I get rid of these boots and pants."

"I'll help." After pulling her legs out from under his, she lithely twisted around, knelt between his legs, and reached for his belt buckle.

"The boots have to come first, Megan," he informed her.

"*You* take care of them. I'm busy."

Although he had to work over her, he quickly unlaced the boots and slipped both them and his socks from his feet. By the time he finished and sat upright again, she'd already finished with the buckle and the snap and turned her attention to his zipper. He wasn't surprised that she was having some difficulty with it; their positioning alone complicated the task, to say nothing of the pressure the zipper was getting from inside his pants. "Megan, darlin', be careful there. Let me get up."

She shook her head obstinately. "I want to do it. Lie down."

Alex shifted his weight and lay flat on his back with his arms at his sides, following orders, for once. In addition to recognizing and responding to the determination in her voice, he perceived it would accomplish the same purpose as standing—as well as, if the expression on her face were an accurate indicator of what she had in mind, being a lot more fun. "Go on ahead then, darlin'. Have your wicked way with me." He grinned at her. "But I'm warning you, it won't be for long."

Megan eased down the zipper, slipped her hand inside, and closed her fingers around him. He was hot and hard and throbbing in her hand and, as she stroked him, she felt a sense of triumphant power that she had finally tumbled the walls that had surrounded his emotions. It was a heady sensation that grew even more powerful when he moaned her name, sounding as if he were in pain. On a sudden impulse to exercise her command over him, she lowered her head, brushing her lips against his flat abdomen and then moving downward.

"No!"

Just that quickly, she was on her back and he was over her again, holding her down with one hand and the weight of his torso while he stripped off his jeans with the other.

"I warned you, Megan," he murmured against her ear. "This time, I want to come inside you, so deep, neither of us can ever forget that you're mine. Is that what you want, too?"

"Yes," she answered with a nod he felt more than saw. "As long as it means that you're mine, too."

"It does, darlin', it does." Lifting his body only enough to maneuver, he skimmed her dress over her head and then glided her panties down her legs and off. Poising himself between her raised knees, he paused a moment and then drove inside her.

She closed her eyes, arched back her neck, and cried out—a sound that made him stop despite his body's demand to go on. She was so tight—which wasn't surprising; by her own admission, she hadn't been with another man since her divorce—he feared he was hurting her. In a harsh whisper, he asked, "Oh, Lord, darlin'... Are you all right? Do you want me to stop?" Even as he made the offer, he couldn't imagine how he'd fulfill it if she told him to do just that.

"It's wonderful," she breathed, opening her eyes and looking up at him as she locked her legs around his waist. "Don't stop. Please don't stop." She lifted her head and touched her mouth to his. "I want more. I want everything.... Give me everything, Alex. All your love, your baby... Please, Alex."

Her last words were almost wailed and the sound of it pierced his heart. Megan with his baby... It was an awesome notion that was scary at the same time that he liked it. He started to move inside her, slowly at first, and then, as she adopted his rhythm and her excitement kept pace with his, with greater and greater fervor. Together, they rushed toward the peak and went over in a burst of sound and flashing lights and sensation that almost exceeded what they thought human beings could endure and survive.

Although his body was weak from his release, Alex bore the brunt of his weight on his arms as he lay over Megan, still inside her and reluctant to leave. He kissed her gently, wondering if she'd heard what he'd said when he climaxed. He'd never told another woman he loved her before. Instead of making him feel weak, as he'd always somehow feared it would, it made him feel stronger, as if he could take on the world and win. And then she opened her eyes and smiled at him, and he felt as if he'd been given an infusion of strength that exceeded even that.

"I heard fireworks," Megan whispered. "Big ones. I saw them, too."

"I hate to disillusion you, but I didn't cause them," he answered with a wry grin. "I think they were from the other side of the island. The festival, remember?"

"Oh. Right."

"But we can try later, and see if they happen again." He rolled off her, and she slid across the narrow mattress to curl tightly against his side. His hand slipped down between them and he eased his body slightly away from hers. "Megan, I'm all sweaty and sticky and ..."

Scooting back into the hollow of his body, Megan countered the objection. "You're *supposed* to be all sweaty and sticky right now, Alex. I am, too. Lesson two: cuddling comes after making love, no matter how sweaty and sticky we are. That's supposed to be half the fun of it. Dammit, Alex, hold me. Tell me again that you love me."

He put his arms around her, trying to ignore the fact that his forearm stuck uncomfortably to her back as if glued there.

"Tell me, Alex."

Lord, she was a tenacious woman. "I love you, Megan."

She smiled and kissed the underside of his jaw. "I love you, too."

Alex settled his head against the top of hers and held her tightly, noticing how the smell of their lovemaking clung to their bodies. It wasn't unpleasant; on the contrary, he liked it—so much so that he found himself becoming aroused again. It surprised him; he wasn't a kid anymore, after all. "Megan, darlin', when was your last period, and are you reasonably regular?"

"Regrets, Alex?"

"No, just curiosity."

"Two weeks ago, just before I went to Umal. And yes, I am."

With a predatory smile, he tightened his arms around her again. "Resign yourself to motherhood, darlin'. I guess this means you'll have to marry me."

"Marry you?" Megan's head shot up off Alex's chest as the words squeaked out and she stared down at him, blinking owlishly.

"Marry me," he repeated firmly, despite the fact that the words had been nearly as much of a surprise to him as they had been to her. Why that was true, he couldn't imagine, after the way he'd felt when Spiro had mentioned marriage and she'd gotten so incensed. The moment the words had left his mouth, he'd known that a commitment, meaning marriage, was the very thing for which he hadn't been willing to wait another five years. Hell, now that he knew what it was he'd been waiting

for, he wasn't sure he could wait even another five *days*.
"I think we should get married as soon as possible."

"Even before we find out whether or not I'm pregnant?"

"By the end of the week, latest."

"*Long* before we find out," she translated.

"It doesn't have a damn thing to do with whether you're pregnant, Megan. Dammit, Megan, if I didn't love you and intend to marry you, we wouldn't even have *discussed* making love without birth control, let alone done it. I'm not letting you get away from me, darlin'." Reaching up, he pulled her back down onto his chest again. "Not again."

"But..." She tried to lift her head, but he held it there.

"I don't know if I'd be able to stand it again, darlin'. I thought it was bad after Florida, but when you ran away from me in Paris, it almost killed me."

"Leaving you almost killed me, too," she admitted.

"So why did you?"

"I was married to Matt then," she said softly, and his arms tightened around her reflexively. "All told, we weren't married very long . . . less than a year, actually. I think we both always knew there was something wrong between us, and when I saw you in Paris, I knew what it was."

"Us?"

"Mmm-hmm." She nodded. "That's why I took off the way I did. I knew then that I'd never be able to forget you. I wanted you so much, and because I was married to Matt, I couldn't have you. So I went back to Delphi—that's where we were at the time—and told him I couldn't stay married to him any longer."

Alex cringed and forced himself to ask the question he wasn't entirely sure he wanted answered, even though the answer was all too apparent to him from everything that had happened in the past week. "Does he know . . . everything?"

"About us? About Florida? Mmm-hmm," Megan confirmed with some embarrassment. Noticing his discomfiture, she insistently added, "Alex, I was married to the man and asking for a divorce. I had to tell him the truth."

"Which is?"

"That I love you, Alex. I always have. As soon as I got back from spring break, I missed you so much, I didn't think I'd be able to stand it."

"I could have found you if you hadn't lied to me."

"I was afraid, Alex! Afraid you wouldn't call, afraid it was nothing more than sex . . ."

"I know that, darlin'," he assured her, shifting beneath her uneasily, feeling responsible for that perception. "Maybe that was my fault. Maybe if I hadn't been so— What were the words you used? Emotionless? Inhuman? Robotic?—you might not have been so uncertain about me."

"Maybe," she replied.

"So will you marry me, then? If I promise to try to show you how I feel? I'm not saying I can change all at once, but . . ."

She lifted her head and smiled down at him. "If you backslide, I can always hit you with a heavy object and remind you."

He smiled back at her. "I think a gentler reminder will be enough."

"Or I can dance with every man at the party again."

He groaned. "Did I really do that? I'm not exactly the kind of man who goes out and drags a woman away from another man, you know."

"As if I couldn't tell."

Alex smiled, his expression smug, filled with pure conquering maleness rather than embarrassment at what he'd done. "Any more than I make a habit of telling one that I want to stay with her always, have children with her."

"Tell her you love her?" Megan prompted with a smile he felt against his chest.

"That, too," he answered before dropping a quick kiss on the top of her head. "Marry me, Megan. Help me try."

"Okay, but you get to be the one to tell my father." She snuggled against him, as if settling in for the night. "We'll go over to the mainland and call my folks tomorrow. Yours, too."

"Do you think Niko'll be up to it by then?" he asked warily, not solely because he was uncertain about the man's prospects for sobriety. He wasn't sure Niko would let him back into the chopper. On the other hand, Niko might, just to throw him out somewhere over the ocean.

"Probably." Recognizing the real source of Alex's anxiety about the pilot, she added, "And I'd be willing to bet he won't even remember what happened tonight. He was *really* drunk. So no squirming out of it, Alex. You get to talk to my father."

"Ask him for his daughter's hand in marriage?"

"It *is* the proper thing to do, you know."

Alex heard the distant sound of the approaching Land Rover and remembered his gear, which was still outside. "Speaking of propriety, sounds like the troops are coming back. I'd better get my stuff before everyone in camp knows I'm in here."

She made a small giggling sound that permeated every cell in his body. "Don't be silly, Alex. They all know *exactly* where you are."

He groaned with embarrassment. Dealing with unbridled emotions was going to take some getting used to; he supposed his father had had it a lot easier than he would, since his mother had never demanded it of him. Not publicly, at least; what happened behind closed doors was anybody's guess. "Did I make an ass out of myself?"

"Mmm-hmm," she confirmed, smiling. "Is it any consolation that I liked it?"

"You *liked* it?"

She nodded. "Real, honest-to-God, out-of-control emotion, Alex. I didn't think I'd ever live to see it, no matter how much I tried."

"I'll show you emotion," he muttered under his breath.

"I certainly hope so."

"Just as soon as I grab my stuff and get it in here."

After giving her another quick kiss that sealed the vow and untangling himself from her, Alex went to the flap, reached out, and dragged the other mattress and sleeping bag inside the tent. He was, by all indications, oblivious to his nudity. Megan certainly wasn't, and when he switched off the light, she groaned in disappointment. Several minutes later, she groaned again—this time with fulfillment.

THE FOLLOWING MORNING, as they left her tent and started toward the cook tent, Megan reached out to take his hand. Acting reflexively rather than through any conscious action, Alex eluded her grasp and she stopped and turned toward him, her eyes blazing with outrage.

"You promised, Alex!" she hissed, looking like a furious cat whose ball of string had just been taken away.

At that moment, he realized what he'd done. "I promised to *try*, Megan," he reminded her, feeling both frustration and chagrin. "I never said it was gonna be easy."

"Can't teach an old dog new tricks, huh?" The blaze of outrage turned to a glimmer of wicked amusement.

"Old?" he challenged softly, his eyes gleaming with memories of the night before as he advanced on her. "Who're you calling old, darlin'? Would an old man be able to hold you all night . . ."

"Probably, if that's all I asked for."

"Make you see fireworks five . . ."

"Six," she corrected automatically.

"Six times," he amended, cocking his eyebrow at her as he slipped his arms around her and pulled her close. "Could an old man make you *beg* him to stop before you died of exhaustion?"

"Who begged whom?"

"Could an old man drag you back in there and start all over again?" He pressed his hips against hers, demonstrating that the proposition was a great deal more than just big talk.

"Very nice, Alex." She moved against him provocatively, hating to disappoint both of them with the reminder that there were other things on the agenda for the day. "But we have to fly over to the mainland, remember? Make phone calls?"

"Oh. Right," he said, the deflation of his mood apparent in his voice...and elsewhere. The telephone call to Megan's father was enough to have that effect. The very idea made Alex nervous with a natural masculine reluctance to face the man whose daughter he had just spent an incredibly erotic night with, in spite of the facts that she was an adult and his intentions were entirely honorable.

Megan felt the uneasiness in him and lifted her head to press her lips to his. "Don't worry about it, Alex. He's not nearly as tough as he seems. He's like you, really. Can't you tell?"

A look of genuine confusion crossed Alex's face, and Megan laughed, confusing him even more.

"Do you mean you *really* don't know?"

"Know what?" Alex breathed uneasily, filled with an ominous foreboding.

"Lord, Alex, you must have been the only one at the Agency who didn't know!"

"Know what?" Alex repeated.

"Frank Baker's my father," she said and then watched as a full range of emotions possessed his face one by one: comprehension, amazement, horror, embarrassment. It was a fascinating phenomenon, one she told herself she'd have to induce on some sort of regular basis in the future.

"So that's why we've been sending people after you all these years?"

She nodded, still laughing. "You don't think he'd let his baby girl get into trouble and stay there, do you?"

"And that's why you knew about the American support for both sides in Zoman?"

She nodded again.

"But . . . your name . . ."

"When I started traveling to do fieldwork, we thought it was safer for me to change my name legally to my mother's maiden name so I could use it on my passport. That way, no one could make the connection and kidnap me for leverage over him."

The explanation made perfect sense to Alex; he knew of several other families in the Agency who had done the same thing, for precisely the same reason. Frank ranked high enough within the intelligence community to make Megan a very attractive target. He just wished someone had mentioned it to him before he'd said all those horrible things to Frank about her. When he made the big announcement that he was going to marry her, Frank was going to hurt himself laughing. Or... "He's gonna kill me, you know. Assuming I can ever face him again, that is."

"Don't be ridiculous, Alex. He already likes you. He's going to be thrilled to have you for a son-in-law. Another Agency man in the family, and all that."

"He's not gonna be thrilled when he becomes a grandfather a little too soon to be decent."

"Actually, I think that'll solidly weight the scales in your favor. He's been after me to settle down and give him a few grandchildren for years." She paused, looking up at him with her head cocked to one side. "Do you really think so?"

"Think he'll kill me? It's a good possibility."

She quickly shook her head. "No, Alex... Just think that we're going to make him a grandfather a little too soon to be decent."

He met her eyes gravely, but she thought she saw something else in his expression, an impression he verified a moment later. "I tried, darlin'. I tried."

# Epilogue

"DAMMIT, MEGAN! What the hell do you think you're doing?" Alex roared as he strode over to the edge of the dig and stood glaring down at her. "I swear to God, if I catch you doing something so utterly stupid again, I'll haul your butt back to your father's house in Washington and you'll sit there and knit until you deliver!"

Ignoring his wrath, Megan smiled up at him radiantly from four feet below and then smacked her lips at him, blowing him a kiss.

He knew precisely what she was trying to do, but he resisted the temptation to laugh and return the kiss, aware it would only encourage her. She couldn't continue hopping in and out of the excavation pit with blithe disregard for both the ladders and her pregnancy, which was now more than five months along. "It won't work this time, darlin', so don't even try...."

"Look what Helmut found!" She held up a chunk of carved stone he scarcely glanced at before dismissing it for the more critical matter of Megan's safety. While she was carrying well, mostly because of her height and long, lean build, she adamantly refused to acknowledge that her balance wasn't quite what it had been only a few weeks before. To say nothing of the fact that the pit was getting deeper every week, as they worked their way from the now exhumed shrine toward where they believed the ritual well had been. It went without saying that they'd probably find it, his leave of absence would run out, and Megan would lose her ability to deny her expanding figure all at about the same time, forcing them to thrash out their options. They wouldn't be able to delay the inevitable altercation any longer.

"Megan..." he growled warningly before levering himself over the edge and down next to her. As it was, there'd already been some rather lively discussion on the matter, and it looked as if final agreement was going to involve compromise, which neither of them was very good at. Frank had mentioned the possibility of assigning him to the Agency's European office. That might work, if they could just figure out whether it would mean Megan was going to accept digs in locations with modern amenities like telephones, or he was going to divide his time between places that didn't and whatever happened to be the nearest real modern city.

"Look, Alex!" she tried again, shaking the object at him with no more success at drawing his attention than she'd had the first time. "Do you know what this is?"

"No, but I know what *this* is." Alex stroked his hand over the hard surface of her belly, another argument in his favor. As far as he knew, Gus "didn't know nothin' 'bout birthin' no babies," and places with telephones usually had real hospitals, too. "And you have to take care of baby until he gets out and can fend for himself."

"Baby is fine, Alex," Megan insisted. Alex was so overprotective, he couldn't recognize that she knew her limits and respected them, no matter how many times she reminded him of that fact. Just as she constantly reminded him, with absolutely no scientific evidence to back her claim that the baby was a girl. "And *she*

wants her mother to make an important discovery before the poor woman's too big to get in and out of the
pit without a hoist."

"Megan . . ."

"Do you know what this is?" she demanded, handing him the object and finally forcing him to look at it.

"It sorta looks like a spigot."

"It *is* a spigot. And I think it's just like the one I saw
in the Zomani National Museum in Tel Mapur...." Her
eyes gleamed with excitement, and he knew, all too
well, what was coming next. "I want to go back and
take another look at it so I can compare them."

Damn woman. *Damn plumbing.* With a sigh of resignation, Alex handed it back to her and put his arms
around her. "When do we leave?"

She lifted her face and kissed the underside of his jaw.
"I love you, Alex."

He sighed again and tightened his arms. "I love you,
too."

"Show me."

He sighed yet again and showed her.

**Earth, Wind, Fire, Water**
**The four elements—but nothing is**
**more elemental than passion**

PASSION'S
QUEST

Join us for Passion's Quest, four sizzling, action-packed
romances in the tradition of *Romancing the Stone* and
*The African Queen*. Starting in January 1994, one book each
month is a sexy, romantic adventure focusing on the quest
for passion, set against the essential elements of earth, wind,
fire and water.

**On sale in March**

March comes in with a roar with Lynn Michaels's *Aftershock*.
The earth moved under her feet...and not only because
Rockie Wexler's father had accidentally created a device that
would cause earthquakes. Rockie's whole world quaked
when she met Dr. Leslie Sheridan. The hard-edged, self-
described pain in the butt was the one man who could help
find her kidnapped father. But Sheridan had his own
reasons for hating anyone with the last name of Wexler....

**The quest continues...**

Coming in April—*Undercurrent* by Lisa Harris.

**Passion's Quest—four fantastic adventures,**
**four fantastic love stories**

HARLEQUIN®
*Temptation*

**Relive the romance...
Harlequin and Silhouette
are proud to present**

 *by Request*™

A program of collections of three complete novels by the most requested authors with the most requested themes. Be sure to look for one volume each month with three complete novels by top name authors.

In January:   **WESTERN LOVING**   Susan Fox
                                                  JoAnn Ross
                                                  Barbara Kaye

*Loving a cowboy is easy—taming him isn't!*

In February:   **LOVER, COME BACK!**   Diana Palmer
                                                        Lisa Jackson
                                                        Patricia Gardner Evans

*It was over so long ago—yet now they're calling, "Lover, Come Back!"*

In March:   **TEMPERATURE RISING**   JoAnn Ross
                                                        Tess Gerritsen
                                                        Jacqueline Diamond

*Falling in love—just what the doctor ordered!*

**Available at your favorite retail outlet.**

REQ-G3

 HARLEQUIN®  *Silhouette*®

# *My Valentine* 1994

Celebrate the most romantic day of the year with
*MY VALENTINE 1994*
a collection of original stories, written by
four of Harlequin's most popular authors...

*MARGOT DALTON*
*MURIEL JENSEN*
*MARISA CARROLL*
*KAREN YOUNG*

*Available in February, wherever
Harlequin Books are sold.*

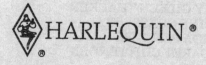

HARLEQUIN®

VAL94

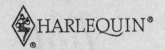

# HARLEQUIN®

# MARRIAGE BY Design

Harlequin proudly presents four stories about
*convenient* but not *conventional* reasons for marriage:

- ◆ To save your godchildren from a
  "wicked stepmother"

- ◆ To help out your eccentric aunt—and her sexy
  business partner

- ◆ To bring an old man happiness by making him
  a grandfather

- ◆ To escape from a ghostly existence and become a
  real woman

Marriage By Design—four brand-new stories by four
of Harlequin's most popular authors:

CATHY GILLEN THACKER
JASMINE CRESSWELL
GLENDA SANDERS
MARGARET CHITTENDEN

Don't miss this exciting collection of stories about
marriages of convenience. Available in April, wherever
Harlequin books are sold.

MBD94

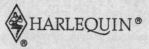

**HARLEQUIN**®

Don't miss these Harlequin favorites by some of our most distinguished authors!
And now, you can receive a discount by ordering two or more titles!

| HT#25409 | THE NIGHT IN SHINING ARMOR by JoAnn Ross | $2.99 | ☐ |
| HT#25471 | LOVESTORM by JoAnn Ross | $2.99 | ☐ |
| HP#11463 | THE WEDDING by Emma Darcy | $2.89 | ☐ |
| HP#11592 | THE LAST GRAND PASSION by Emma Darcy | $2.99 | ☐ |
| HR#03188 | DOUBLY DELICIOUS by Emma Goldrick | $2.89 | ☐ |
| HR#03248 | SAFE IN MY HEART by Leigh Michaels | $2.89 | ☐ |
| HS#70464 | CHILDREN OF THE HEART by Sally Garrett | $3.25 | ☐ |
| HS#70524 | STRING OF MIRACLES by Sally Garrett | $3.39 | ☐ |
| HS#70500 | THE SILENCE OF MIDNIGHT by Karen Young | $3.39 | ☐ |
| HI#22178 | SCHOOL FOR SPIES by Vickie York | $2.79 | ☐ |
| HI#22212 | DANGEROUS VINTAGE by Laura Pender | $2.89 | ☐ |
| HI#22219 | TORCH JOB by Patricia Rosemoor | $2.89 | ☐ |
| HAR#16459 | MACKENZIE'S BABY by Anne McAllister | $3.39 | ☐ |
| HAR#16466 | A COWBOY FOR CHRISTMAS by Anne McAllister | $3.39 | ☐ |
| HAR#16462 | THE PIRATE AND HIS LADY by Margaret St. George | $3.39 | ☐ |
| HAR#16477 | THE LAST REAL MAN by Rebecca Flanders | $3.39 | ☐ |
| HH#28704 | A CORNER OF HEAVEN by Theresa Michaels | $3.99 | ☐ |
| HH#28707 | LIGHT ON THE MOUNTAIN by Maura Seger | $3.99 | ☐ |

## *Harlequin Promotional Titles*

| #83247 | YESTERDAY COMES TOMORROW by Rebecca Flanders | $4.99 | ☐ |
| #83257 | MY VALENTINE 1993 | $4.99 | ☐ |

(short-story collection featuring Anne Stuart, Judith Arnold,
Anne McAllister, Linda Randall Wisdom)

**(limited quantities available on certain titles)**

|  | AMOUNT | $ |
| DEDUCT: | 10% DISCOUNT FOR 2+ BOOKS | $ |
| ADD: | POSTAGE & HANDLING | $ |
|  | ($1.00 for one book, 50¢ for each additional) | |
|  | APPLICABLE TAXES* | $ _____ |
|  | TOTAL PAYABLE | $ _____ |
|  | (check or money order—please do not send cash) | |

To order, complete this form and send it, along with a check or money order for the total above, payable to Harlequin Books, to: **In the U.S.:** 3010 Walden Avenue, P.O. Box 9047, Buffalo, NY 14269-9047; **In Canada:** P.O. Box 613, Fort Erie, Ontario, L2A 5X3.

Name: _____

Address: _____ City: _____

State/Prov.: _____ Zip/Postal Code: _____

*New York residents remit applicable sales taxes.
Canadian residents remit applicable GST and provincial taxes.

HBACK-JM